Books by Genevieve Fox

ARMY SURGEON

CYNTHIA OF BEE TREE HOLLOW

MOUNTAIN GIRL

MOUNTAIN GIRL COMES HOME

BONNIE, ISLAND GIRL

Bonnie, Island Girl

by GENEVIEVE FOX

Bonnie,
Island Girl

Illustrated by
Mary Morton Weissfeld

LITTLE, BROWN AND COMPANY
Boston

Published simultaneously
in Canada by McClelland and Stewart Limited

PRINTED IN THE UNITED STATES OF AMERICA

TO
*Ruth, Mary Jean
and Sally*

Contents

Bonnie, Island Girl

1. Bonnie Graduates

BONNIE Jean Andrews!"

A fourteen-year-old girl jumped up like a released spring, crossed the platform and took from the school superintendent's outstretched hand a white-ribbon-tied roll of paper. She walked carefully to keep from stepping on her long white dress, the first long skirt she had ever worn. She held her small head stiffly to keep a paper crown from toppling off her dark curls. Her eyes were diamond-bright. Her cheeks burned.

No wonder Bonnie was excited. This small roll of paper meant that her school days on Bayberry Island were over. Never again would she take the path across Cranberry Point to the small white schoolhouse at the call of the morning bell. In September she must leave home and go to high school *on the mainland.*

To add to the evening's excitement, she had played the lead in the school operetta — a queen who wore a gilt crown and a necklace that sparkled just like the real thing — and she had sung a long solo and been clapped back three times.

The Bayberry Harbor Town Hall was crowded with men, women, children and babies. They had come from all over the island to see the graduation exercises. Of the many pairs of eyes now fastened on her, Bonnie was conscious of only three. One pair, as dark and almost as shining as her own, was her mother's. The gray ones with many lines at the corners from squinting at sunlit water were her father's. The third pair, the color of the sea in June, belonged to a light-haired boy a couple of years older than she, who grinned up at her from the back row.

4

Diplomas were given to the three other members of the class. The evening was over. Friends and relatives crowded around Bonnie. Her cheeks grew still brighter as she listened to the nice things they said —

"Oh Bonnie, you were wonderful!"

"Some queen!"

"You sang fine."

"We were proud of you, dear." Her mother said that.

Jimmy Daniels, the blue-eyed boy in the back row, did not join the group around the girl graduate. Yet when she came out he was waiting at the door. For a moment he seemed on the point of telling her how pretty she looked. But he only said, "Hi, Queen Bonnie, better take that crown off your head 'fore it falls off." Then — "Rowed over in my new skiff. Thought you'd like a ride home."

Dave and Billy, the nine-year-old twins, came running after their older sister. Jimmy waved a commanding hand toward the path across Cranberry Point. "You kids can walk. This is Bonnie's night."

It was less than a quarter of a mile from the village of Bayberry Harbor across Cranberry Point to Pretty Cove. But tonight the girl graduate was not dressed for walking. And Jimmy, the boatbuilder, wanted to show off his skiff.

5

The long northern summer day was not quite over when they walked down to the beach. Across the west stretched a pinkish-gold band tinting the satiny water. But to the east the moon rode above dark water and the shapes of the rocks alongshore had begun to blur. A few last straggling gulls flew with swift wingbeats to their roosting places.

"It's a beauty," she told the boy as he pushed the graceful skiff off, jumped in and handled the oars with a practiced hand.

"Not bad for the first one, I guess. What you s'pose I'm going to do this summer?"

"Work in the cannery at Easton?"

"Not me. Got me a job in Murphy's boatshop over there. He's building a sixty-foot seiner."

"You'll love that."

"*I'll* say."

The girl was silent. She thought how simple Jimmy's life would be. He knew exactly where he was going. He wanted to build boats, had wanted to ever since he could whittle out toy schooners with a jackknife. As for herself, there were so many things she wanted to do. Sometimes she thought she'd be a nurse, perhaps an army nurse. Last summer, after talking with Alice Lee Hanover, who wrote books and had a summer cottage on the other side of the

6

island, she decided to be a writer. Tonight, having had a taste of being a prima donna, she dreamed of singing and acting, maybe on the radio or on television.

"Oh Jimmy, just think. Next year I'll be living in Broad Harbor and going to school there." Her voice went up the scale excitedly. To leave the island and live in a good-sized mainland town that she'd seen only once, to go to a school with two or three hundred others — that seemed a tremendous experience. There had never been more than twenty-five at the island school and all of them boys and girls who had grown up together. Just to think about the fifth of September gave her a fluttery feeling inside.

"At first," said Jimmy, "it'll be about like trying to row around Cranberry in a northeaster."

"Why?"

"Because it'll all be so different from Bayberry Island. Anyway, I felt like that when I went to Easton."

Jimmy, who was sixteen, had been going to high school for two years down-coast at Easton, where his uncle and aunt lived.

"I remember how mixed up I was and how the guys down there tried to put things over on me and get my goat. They thought because I'd always lived

7

on an island I didn't know my way round. I had to show them — with my fists."

"You make it sound awful."

"Oh, I guess it'll be different for a girl. But don't expect to be the brightest and most popular girl in school and leading lady in plays and everything, like you've been here."

"Why *not?*"

"Competition. Lots of it."

Yes, everything would be different now. But she'd *show* those mainland boys and girls that Bonnie Jean Andrews from Bayberry Island knew her way around. If only somebody else from here were going to Broad Harbor! The four graduates were scattering — Mary Lunt to Bellport because she could live with her cousin there; George Murray to South Point High because he had heard of a job down there where he could work evenings. Ted Green, the other member of her class, was through school and was going to work on his father's seiner. It sure would be queer not to have anybody around who even *looked* familiar.

The boy at the oars was now busy with thoughts of his own future. "In two years I'll be going off someplace — probably Boston. I want to learn how to design and build boats — everything about 'em. Guess Boston'll seem different all right."

8

"We won't see much of you here after that."

"Why *not?* I'll always come back to Bayberry. When I have my own boatshop it's going to be on Bayberry — near Bayberry, anyway."

"It *will?*"

"Sure! Wouldn't live anyplace else."

In the dusk he could not see her disbelieving smile. Once he'd gone to the city he'd take a good job and never come back. That was what always happened when an island boy went away.

They rounded Cranberry Point, a dark finger of rock that reached out to the sea between the village of Bayberry Harbor and Pretty Cove. The boat grated on the strip of pebbly beach. They climbed the steep dirt path to the cluster of small houses perched above the rocks against black woods, and stopped at the door of a little box of a white house.

A variety of noises floated out through the open windows. From one of the two downstairs rooms a short-wave radio gave out unnatural squawking sounds. Pa had sat down as usual the minute he got home to listen to the herring and mackerel fishermen calling each other from boat to boat all up and down the coast by radiotelephone. It was better than a newspaper as far as fishing news was concerned.

Jerry Thomas calling the Mary K. *Over.*

9

The Mary K. *calling the* Sea Breeze. *Come in,*
Jerry.

Not much of a run here tonight, George. I'm going
down to Brady's Cove.

Out of the kitchen window came the small sounds
that Ma made as she did last things — laid a wood
fire in the kitchen stove ready to light in the morning,
set out on the oilcloth-covered table the things Pa
would need to eat his five-o'clock breakfast before
starting out on the round of his lobster traps. Upstairs
there were the thumps and squeals of good-natured
tussles and pillow fights, as the three younger children got ready for bed.

The boy and girl stopped before the never-used
front door. Almost instantly two heads popped out of
the small window above and two snickering boys
looked down on them. "Hi, Bonnie! Hi, Jimmy!
Takes a long time to row from the Harbor, don't
it?"

Would there ever be a time, Bonnie wondered,
when she could talk with Jimmy or any other boy
without those two kids popping up or out from someplace to listen in. They were like her shadows.

"Well, good night, Bonnie. Be seeing you."

"Good night, Jimmy."

In a few moments she heard his boat splash as he

shoved it off and headed back to Bayberry Harbor, where he lived.

She was the last person in the house to go to sleep that night. Five-year-old Betty lay in the bed beside her, limp as the dirty rag doll she cuddled. The scufflings and thumpings from the next room, where the boys slept, ceased. The cracked voices on the radio were silenced abruptly. She heard the bump-bump downstairs of the folding couch being opened up into a bed by her mother.

In a few minutes the only sounds to be heard were the *swish-swash, swish-swash* of the waves breaking against the rocks and now and then the "Qwok" of a night heron as he watched with eyes that could see in the dark for fish.

Still Bonnie was wide-awake. Songs from the operetta went round and round inside her head. The nice things people had said to her that evening repeated themselves, also what Jimmy had told her about high school on the mainland. She understood now what people meant when they talked about turning points in their lives. This graduation was a turning point for her.

The moon poured white light through the one window under the eaves. It made a shimmering path on the water. That watery path seemed to lead right out across the ocean from Maine to — Let's see, the coast of France must be out there. Some day perhaps she would go to France and to other faraway places. She wouldn't just stay on an island all her life.

If she sailed out that moonlit trail it would keep lengthening, lengthening. On second thought, she wouldn't sail. She would fly right up under the moon in a shining plane.

Bonnie slept.

2. Interrupted Plans

THE long June days seemed to Bonnie the shortest of the year: they were so full of plans and preparations. She and her mother pored over mail-order catalogues. They made a list of things the girl absolutely must have before going to high school. A new coat, two pairs of new shoes, one good dress, a new skirt, a sweater — these were musts. So was a new suitcase to put them in.

"There's a little over a hundred dollars in the Harbor Savings Bank. That ought to take care of anything you have to buy. I'll make you some slips and nighties and you can knit yourself a pretty sweater."

"I'll knit a red one just the shade of my new bag," Bonnie planned. She had had a bright red handbag for a graduation present, sent her by Aunt Elizabeth and Uncle Arthur from Massachusetts. She kept the gift all wrapped up in tissue paper in her bureau drawer, but took it out often and swung it on her arm before the tiny looking glass in her room. Her sweater must be just that color, with perhaps a beanie to go with it. Maybe, *maybe,* she could have red shoes too.

Clothes for the high-school freshman were important. Yet there was a still more pressing matter to attend to. Where was she going to live in Broad Harbor? She had to find a room. That might sound fairly simple. It was really complicated. It must be a room she could pay for by baby-sitting or helping about the house in some way.

"Tomorrow morning you and I'll take the mail boat for Broad Harbor and look around for a place," Ma announced one day near the end of June. "Grace McAdam says she knows a Mrs. Ellis over there who isn't very well and wants to find a nice girl to live in the house and help her a little. We'd better go before she gets somebody else."

Bonnie washed her hair and washed and ironed her prettiest blouse for the trip. "Call me at six," she told

14

her mother when she went to bed. The mail boat left Bayberry Harbor at seven.

They did not take the boat that day. Nobody called Bonnie at six. She rushed downstairs at six-thirty, all dressed up for the trip, to find her mother lying very still on the folding bed in the living room.

"Are you sick, Ma?"

The head on the pillow nodded slightly. Ma's voice, when she spoke, was faint and tired-sounding. She didn't want any breakfast, not even a cup of tea.

Bonnie fixed something for herself and the younger children, washed up the dishes, then went back to the figure on the bed.

The woman lying there didn't look like her mother, she realized suddenly. All the bright color was gone from her face. It was grayish-white now — and gone, too, were the lights from the dark eyes.

"Do you feel awful, Ma?"

She nodded as if with a great effort.

"Want me to get Emma McKay to come?" Emma was a practical nurse who lived at the Harbor.

"I — I guess I need a doctor," she murmured, and kept her eyes closed so that Bonnie might not see the pain in them.

A doctor! Oh, she must be terribly sick. There was no doctor on Bayberry Island.

15

"I'll get one," the girl said, then added under her breath — "*somehow.*"

Going to the kitchen door, she called to the three children playing on the strip of sand in the Cove, "Dave, Billy, Betty, come quick!"

They rushed into the house with the force of a tidal wave but quieted suddenly when they saw their sister's face. "Ma's pretty sick," she whispered. "I'm going over to the Harbor and send for a doctor if I can. You stay near the house so you can hear Ma if she wants something. I'll be back in a few minutes."

She was off on a run, even forgetting to take off her apron.

"I'll get a doctor," she had said — just like that, as if it were a perfectly simple thing to do. Yet how many chances out of a hundred did she have of sending any word to the mainland before afternoon? The mail boat had left more than an hour ago. All the fishing boats would be out. Yet she *had* to get help for Ma quick. Nobody needed to tell her that. She had seen it in the gray face. All at once something heavy seemed to be lying on her shoulders, weighing her down.

Bonnie ran till she came to the woods and out into Johnson's pasture. From this open hillside one looked down on the village, the harbor and out to a flock of small islands, and could see, a half hour before they reached the landing, the incoming boats as they picked their way among those islands.

The girl stood still on the hilltop and scanned the expanse of water where the men moored their boats. Empty blue space met her eyes — empty, that is, except for the dories and canoe-shaped "pea-pods" bobbing up and down there, and for a few brightly painted lobster buoys marking the location of some near-shore traps. The little harbor seemed to sleep under the morning sun. Only the ever-watchful gulls were awake.

What to do now!

For several seconds Bonnie just stood there, her legs and thinking apparatus paralyzed. Then she began desperately trying to plan. Should she wait on the dock a few minutes and see if some boat might come in? Yet every minute was precious. Should she see if Captain Otis was down in his boat-repair shop? He'd know if anyone was likely to be coming into the harbor soon.

Just as she had decided to go to see the captain a miracle from heaven happened. At least it seemed a miracle then, and always would, to Bonnie. Out from behind Seal Island a sturdy boat appeared, a boat with a gray hull. Could it — *could* it be the *Sunbeam?*

She put up her hand for an eyeshade and stared across the sunlit water till her eyeballs hurt. Yes. A white cross gleamed against the dark prow. The Sea Coast Mission boat was coming! — the boat that plied up and down the coast and among the islands to help people in out-of-the-way, out-of-touch places at just such times as these!

Was the *Sunbeam* coming into the harbor? she asked the next moment. Or was it heading down the coast? Impossible to tell yet. Could they see her if she signaled? She went running down the hill and out to the end of the dock. There she stood and waved her mother's apron like a blue and white banner high above her head. Those few desperate minutes while she signaled and waited seemed an hour. Not till the gray prow was pointed straight toward her could Bonnie be certain that the skipper was making for Bayberry Harbor landing. It was the most beautiful sight she had ever seen — that boat cutting quickly through the water, the white cross on its prow growing larger all the time.

There followed a day of waiting.

Bonnie waited for the *Sunbeam* to come in to Bayberry Harbor. She waited for the *Sunbeam* to round Cranberry Point, then put in and anchor in Pretty Cove. She waited while the skiff came ashore. She

18

waited while her mother was carried on a stretcher down the path to the skiff and out to the Mission boat. She waited and watched while the boat with the white cross disappeared behind Cranberry Point, carrying her mother away to the mainland — *to the hospital*. In the afternoon she waited for her father to come home.

He had left at five-thirty that morning with no idea that Ma was very sick. No matter how worried he would be when he knew, he would be calm and quiet. Pa was always like that. And Bonnie longed for someone calm to talk to. The children were excited. They kept asking if Ma was awful sick and where were those folks taking her and what were they going to do to her and when was she coming back. The neighbors were anxious and full of questions and so sympathetic they made the children all the more worried. Elderly Mrs. Joyce wanted to come in and cook their supper, but Bonnie said she had enough left-over lobster stew for another meal. Mrs. McAdam asked Betty to come over to her house and play with three-year-old Sam. The little girl could not have been pried apart from her older sister.

Mabel Collins fired questions like a machine gun — Didn't their Ma look awful? What was the matter with her? What would they do to her at the hospital?

19

Did she have to have her appendix or something took out like Lizzie Joyce did?

At fifteen, Mabel was still a little child who went about saying anything that came into her mind, listening in on conversations, repeating everything she heard to the next person she met and oftener than not getting it all mixed up. From her listening and watching post at the small grocery store which Mrs. Collins kept in her home — the only store in Pretty Cove — Mabel saw and heard just about everything that went on in the small settlement.

Even after she ran out of inquiries about Mrs. Andrews, Mabel continued to hang around within watching distance. Apparently she expected lightning to strike the Andrews house at any moment and wanted to be on hand when it did.

Long before their father could possibly have hauled all his traps, the four children went out on Cranberry Point to watch for him and listen for the first distant throbbing of his boat, the *Anne Marie*, named for Ma. The voice of that boat was different to their ears from the voice of any of the other fishing boats that went out at dawn and came back at the end of day. The *Anne Marie* did not purr like a boat with a big, powerful engine. Neither was she a put-putter or a tinny clatterer like some of the other lobster boats. It always seemed to Bonnie that she hummed a song as she headed in to Pretty Cove.

At last a boat slid out between Goose Island and Seal Island. From Cranberry Point it looked no bigger than a lobster pot. The youngsters stood on the farthest rock and watched the craft grow bigger and bigger and listened. "It's the *Anne Marie!*" they chorused. Chummy, the mongrel terrier, let out a delighted bark as they all went pelting back to Pretty Cove. The four stood at the very water's edge while their father dropped anchor at his mooring, climbed into the small boat tied to the stern and rowed ashore. This all seemed to take a long time today.

"What's the matter?" he called while still several yards from the beach. One look at that row of faces told him something was quite wrong at Pretty Cove.

Billy blurted everything right out. "Ma went to the hospital on the *Sunbeam*. She was terrible sick."

"What hospital?" Mr. Andrews demanded.

"Broad Harbor. They said she *had* to go," explained Bonnie vaguely.

At once her father began backing water. "I'm going over there!" he shouted as he turned the boat around. "Don't look for me before tomorrow noon anyway. Listen to the radio, Bonnie, and I'll get some word to you this evening if I can."

21

He rowed back to the mooring in half the time he had come ashore.

Bonnie's face was even more sober than it had been before. She'd have to be calm and quiet without any help from anybody. She'd have to be head of the family tonight.

"Come on, kids. Let's have supper. There's lobster stew and apple pie." She spoke with artificial cheerfulness. She felt no enthusiasm for eating lobster or anything else.

Not till the fragrance of the hot, buttery stew rose from the kitchen stove did the girl remember that she had eaten nothing but a few berries since breakfast and realize that she was faint for want of food.

The twins wanted to sit up and listen to the radio. "I won't go to bed till Dave and Billy do," insisted Betty. "I'm not going to stay upstairs all alone."

Bonnie looked into the three anxious faces and decided to let the youngsters sit up as long as they could keep awake. They perched on the couch in a row, determinedly stiff and straight, and listened to the voices coming over the air from the boats. Presently the monotonous sounds set their heads to nodding. First, Betty's went sideways, then Dave's pitched forward and straightened up quickly, only to nod forward again. By nine o'clock all three were ready to stumble upstairs.

The kitchen clock struck nine-thirty, then ten and ten-thirty. Bonnie still sat close to the radio, listening tensely. Still those unearthly voices went on, but they talked only of soundings here, soundings there, where they were filling nets with mackerel and where they had found none, where the herring were running.

The Sea Rover *in Broad Harbor calling . . .*

At the words "Broad Harbor" the girl jumped out of her chair. Was this Pa's message coming through?

The Sea Rover *just outside Broad Harbor calling the* Puffin.

The Puffin *off Seal Rock Light calling the* Sea Rover. *Come in.*

Bonnie drew in her breath quickly and held it.

That you, Sam? This is John Hawkes. Not much of a run here. Pete Andrews wants to let his kids know that their mother is pretty comfortable. He'll be back tomorrow sometime or else he'll send a message again. Over.

Bonnie dropped down on the couch with her clothes on, pulled up the knitted afghan that lay across the foot of it and knew nothing more till the twins and Betty clattered down the stairs next morning calling, "Bonnie! Bonnie! Aren't you up *yet?*"

3. Waiting for Ma to Come Home

THE little house in Pretty Cove seemed empty. Yet it had never been so full — full of restlessness. Chummy wandered about, sniffing here and there, scratching at the kitchen door to come in, only to whine to be let out again. Betty stayed in the house as long as Bonnie did, following her from the kitchen to the living room and back, to the woodshed and back, up and down stairs. The twins, who could usually play by themselves for hours, were as bothersome as Chummy. They ran in and out of the house.

24

They scuffled. They knocked over the furniture. They teased Betty. They kept asking Bonnie to tell them again "what Pa said over the radio."

"He said Ma was pretty comfortable," she repeated more cheerfully than she felt, wondering all the time what he meant by "pretty comfortable." If their mother really was better, why was he so uncertain about when he would get back? She wished the day away. Yet she dreaded its end and the news it might bring from Broad Harbor.

Right after noonday dinner she suggested, to the younger children's delight, that they go to Secret Cove. This was their special place, their refuge when life got tough or boring. The narrow cove was no secret. Yet almost no one except the Andrews children ever bothered to go there. On the ocean side it was walled by steep rocks, with an entrance so narrow only a small rowboat could reach the bit of a beach at the head of the inlet. To reach the cove from the shore side meant plunging into a deep spruce woods, then through a briery thicket, leaping from hummock to hummock across a mucky swamp and through another strip of woods. It was, they thought, worth all the effort. Nowhere else were there such fascinating things to do, such beachcombing, and such a feeling of privacy. There was even a great spruce that leaned out over the narrow beach, with low-hanging branches like curtains.

Today the small cove seemed to hold out its arms to the restless youngsters. Betty settled down at once to play house in the old wrecked dory wedged between two rocks. The boys gathered treasures — beautiful, sea-bleached boards to take home for amateur building operations, bottles and shells and stones, a bottomless, headless cask to crawl through and play "train going into tunnel." In their island lives they had never seen trains — only pictures of them, which made the game all the more exciting.

Bonnie too felt more peaceful here than at home. She leaned back into a hollowed-out rock that was like a chair under the spruce tree and read a mystery story borrowed from the Harbor library.

Presently the boys had an idea — for something they had never thought of doing before. They would build a dam of rocks across the end of the inlet and make a quiet pool where they could sail toy boats. In a few minutes Betty caught their enthusiasm and suspended housekeeping to lug rocks for the dam. Finally Bonnie got so interested she left her story at an exciting place and waded into the water to help. They worked away till the sun was dropping into the pointed tops of the spruces and firs. They kept at it till the dam was done. Then their imaginations started on the pool.

"Why don't you bring over the little lighthouse Pa whittled for you?" suggested Bonnie to the boys.

"Yeah, and build some little houses and have lots of little boats," they chimed in.

"We could make a regular fishing village," she went on.

"What'll we call it?" asked one.

They decided on Andrews Village. Now more than ever the inlet was their own place.

"I shall play with Cap'n Hill's little girl," announced Betty.

"*Whose?*"

"Cap'n Hill's. He's the lighthouse keeper and he's got a little girl just my age." Already she was peopling the village with a captain and a captain's daughter.

It was almost dark in the spruce woods when they ran home. Still they had seen or heard no sign of the *Anne Marie.*

"I've had the radio on all afternoon and ain't heard nothing from your father," Mrs. Joyce called to them from her back door. "But no news is good news, you know."

Why did people say that? No news could be anything, absolutely *anything*, thought Bonnie.

The first thing she did when she went into the house was to turn on their own radio. She listened while she prepared supper and while she ate supper and as she washed the dishes. When work in the kitchen was done, the four of them sat down as they had the night before to listen again to the queer-sounding voices that went on and on. Somehow those voices seemed to be mocking at them tonight.

Bonnie looked more and more like a worried owl, her face all eyes. The twins were two solemn little old men sitting beside her. Even Betty's blue eyes were dark and big, and there were rings under them. Bonnie found herself wishing that they would scuffle and knock things over, even fight. Anything would be better than this awful gravity. It was past their bedtime, yet she knew there was no use sending them to bed.

Suddenly Chummy leaped up and began to yelp.

A dazzling light shone for a moment into the front windows. A bright pathway reached out across the dark water. A boat was coming! Then three blasts of the whistle sounded. It was the *Anne Marie*. Pa would never blow the whistle like that unless it was good news. In a few seconds they were down on the beach.

"She's getting along fine. She's going to be all right." So long as she lived Bonnie would never forget the comfort of those words coming out of the darkness as her father rowed ashore. Their mother had been mighty sick but she was out of danger now, he told them as he beached the dory. However, she'd have to stay in the hospital for two weeks, the doctor said, and then take life pretty easy for a while.

Fourteen whole days without Ma! It seemed an endless length of time as those days stretched ahead. Yet the two weeks rushed by, there were so many things to do. First of all, they wanted to have their village in Secret Cove all done to show to her. They could row her around and she could sit in the stone armchair, and wouldn't she be surprised though! A family of beavers never worked harder than those four did on Andrews Village. When they were not busy there the twins were hammering away at home, sawing, whittling, wielding a paint brush.

On Saturday Jimmy, who worked in Easton now, put-putted into Pretty Cove to show off the new outboard motor he had attached to his skiff. He was at once escorted through the woods and across the swamp to the village. It now boasted a lighthouse, gay with red and white paint, two tiny cottages painted to match the lighthouse, a boat landing, two red sailboats, whittled out by the twins with help from Pa, with sails made by their older sister.

"Sa-ay, that's sharp!" was Jimmy's verdict. "And I've got some things to make it sharper. Be right back."

In a few minutes they heard the sputtering of his boat as it started for the Harbor. They waited in a state of excitement. What could he be bringing them? He reappeared in a few minutes with something held high in each hand.

"Whatcha got? Whatcha got?" they cried impatiently.

"Boat models. Mr. Murphy gave them to me. Guess I can get some more too. Every boat they build has a model like that."

The proprietors of Andrews Village just stood and stared. Here were perfect miniatures of real fishing boats — a dragger and a seiner — complete with masts, steering wheels, anchors, port and starboard lanterns and lantern boards — everything.

Betty was the first to speak. "One of the boats is Cap'n Bailey's and the other's Cap'n Swan's and they both have little girls five years old."

Now another enthusiastic worker joined the construction gang at Secret Cove. Jimmy spent all that Saturday afternoon helping to anchor the boats and starting to build, with small sticks and string nets, an exact small-sized copy of a herring weir.

Waiting for Ma to Come Home

Suddenly there were only three days left before Ma would be coming home. Bonnie washed and cleaned till each of the four rooms shone. The floors were spotless and dustless. The windowpanes sparkled and the curtains at the windows were as white as a gull's breast.

Two days more.

One day more!

"Tomorrow! Tomorrow! Ma's coming home tomorrow!" sang Betty to a little tune of her own when she got out of bed that Saturday morning. She sang her song at intervals all day, as everyone hustled about preparing for the event. She and Bonnie upholstered the rock chair at Secret Cove with moss so that it would be soft for their mother to sit on. Pa scrubbed out his lobster boat. One might have eaten a meal off the bottom when he was through.

4. A Family Again

THERE was no sleeping late that Sunday morning. The whole family was up by the time the sun had climbed over the pointed treetops behind the house.

The twins and Betty picked armfuls of daisies, red clover, buttercups, devil's-paintbrush and old-fashioned roses from the bush by the front door. Bonnie filled glasses, pitchers and milk bottles with the flowers and brought the summer into the living room.

Pa collected cushions and pillows and took them

out to the *Anne Marie* to make a soft place where the convalescent could lie down. Too impatient to stay at home, he set out at six o'clock.

"And now," announced Bonnie, when the house looked as if it were ready for a wedding, "you boys have got to have haircuts. Billy, sit down here by the window. I'll start with you." Clapping a good-sized bowl down over his light-brown head, she began snipping off his hair, following the rim of the bowl just as she had seen her mother do it. The job was not as easy as it had looked when Ma wielded the scissors.

"Ouch!" screeched Billy. "Ouch! Ouch!"

"Stop wriggling!" commanded his sister. "I can't help sticking the scissors into your neck when you don't sit still."

Dave, when his turn came, seemed trying to out-wriggle and outscreech his brother.

When she finished, neither twin had the nice even line around his neck that Ma could snip. There were notches and scallops, though she had held the bowl firm and cut close to it.

Everything was ready hours before their mother could possibly arrive, and all four were washed, combed and dressed in clean clothes. Bonnie even had dinner partly ready. To make the time go faster and to see the *Anne Marie* the minute she came out from behind Seal Island, they went to the end of Cranberry Point. There they perched like a row of gulls and waved to every boat that came by.

"Here we come! Here we come!" a boat's engine seemed to sing. It was a lobster boat with two people in it. The figure in the stern waved gaily to them. Four arms of assorted lengths waved back like windmills in a gale.

Ma looked much better than Bonnie had expected her to. There was the old sparkle in her eyes and even a hint of color in her face. As for her smile, it seemed to the children like sunlight breaking through after a long, heavy fog. The chief difference between the woman who had gone away two weeks before and the one who came back was in the fit of her clothes. The belt of the print dress Bonnie had sent over for her to wear home looked as if it would fall down over her hips at any moment. Her light sweater lay in folds across her shoulders and lapped over in front. It could have held two of Mrs. Andrews.

The neighbors joined in the welcome. The Joyces and McAdams called "Hi, Anna! Welcome home!" Even Sammy McAdam and the year-old baby waved welcomes. Mabel Collins came on a run.

There was a complete circle around the dinner table again. Bonnie didn't have to serve. Ma was back in her old place, seeing that everybody had enough. They all ate heartily, including Betty, whose appetite had been noticeably small ever since her mother went away. Chummy was the picture of content, sitting as close as he could get to Mrs. Andrews, with his head pressed against her knee.

It was like Christmas, thought Bonnie. Not that corn hake and potato were a holiday feast. But they sat around the table talking after they had finished eating and they laughed a great deal just as if it were a big holiday. There was such a lot to talk about, so many things they had saved up to tell Ma when she came home: that Mrs. Joyce wanted one of Butterball's kittens — the yellow and white one — and that Mabel Collins wanted the all-yellow one, that the young song sparrows were hatched out in their nest in the small fir tree, that Ben Green had a new dory and last of all that they had something very special to show her tomorrow if she felt like a short boat ride. **U. S. 836446**

They were a family again.

Bonnie's shoulders felt light. So did her heart. Everything would be all right now.

Next morning, after seeing that long list of instructions from the doctor, she felt less carefree. She had to see that the patient rested and rested, that she had lots of good food, with eggnogs, fruit juices and things between meals, and that she didn't worry about anything. In other words Bonnie was elected nurse, housekeeper and also Chief Family Shock Absorber.

Then, about a fortnight later, the girl suddenly asked herself two questions: "Can Ma possibly be well enough by September to carry on by herself? Will I have to give up school?"

Those questions grew louder and louder in her ears as the days went by. They seemed to be shouted at her during that discouraging time when Ma overdid and had a long setback. Bonnie thought she concealed her worries beautifully. Mrs. Andrews, however, was a mind reader when it came to her own children. In a few days she had guessed what her older daughter was thinking about, and did some thinking herself. Then she sat down and wrote to her sister, who lived on Long Island, a large island out beyond Black and Seal.

The answer relieved tension. "If I am not all well by the first of September — and I probably will be — your Aunt Grace will come over and take care of us," Ma announced.

The next thing was to find a place to live in Broad Harbor. The lady who had been looking for a "nice girl" had found one, Mrs. McAdam said. Nice girls,

A Family Again

Bonnie decided, were not scarce. Soon the word *August* would be staring out at her from the calendar above the kitchen table. And August was certainly the shortest month in the year, even if it did have thirty-one days. It was high time to find that room! And she would have to go by herself. How *did* a girl go about it? She pictured herself walking up and down the unfamiliar streets of Broad Harbor, ringing doorbells and asking perfect strangers if she could live with them.

Now Mrs. Andrews had an idea. "You write to that nice Miss Bradley from the Mission. She came to see me in the hospital and I guess she knows about everybody in Broad Harbor."

Next morning the mail boat carried Bonnie's letter. A week went by. No reply came. Then, one morning, a smiling, bright-eyed young woman came swinging along the path across Cranberry Point from Bayberry Harbor. "Is this where Bonnie Andrews lives?" she asked.

Bonnie, who was hanging out clothes in the yard, did not need to be told who the visitor was. "Ma," she called as she opened the door for the caller, "here's the lady from the Mission."

"She'll know just what I should do," the girl said to herself. At least that was the feeling this young woman gave her — she was one of those wonderful people who would always know what to do.

Miss Bradley did have a suggestion, also the name of a person who wanted to find "just such a girl as Bonnie is," though Bonnie couldn't see how this stranger could tell so quickly what kind of girl she really was. Miss Bradley said that Mrs. Barnes would be a "nice person for Bonnie to live with," whatever that meant. She could have her room and breakfasts and a chance to cook her dinners in exchange for baby-sitting with a four-year-old and a two-year-old.

After Ma had asked a number of questions and those questions had been answered to her satisfaction, "Bonnie," she said, "I guess you'd better take it."

The girl thought so too, even sight unseen. The time grew short.

At last everything was settled, she decided.

Bonnie was wrong. Within a week another obstacle rose in her path. This one seemed insurmountable.

5. Just One Thing after Another

BONNIE stopped short on her way downstairs that August morning and listened. Her mother and father were talking together in the kitchen.

"Oh Peter, we can't spend that money we saved for Bonnie. She . . ."

"Got to pay our bills. You couldn't help getting sick. I couldn't help my engine breaking down and having to be fixed or lobsters dropping to thirty cents."

"But a girl can't go away to school without . . ."

"Bonnie'll have to wait a year."

"I'd rather cut out my tongue than tell her that."

"I'll tell her." The kitchen door shut behind him. Mr. Andrews was off for a day on the *Anne Marie*.

The girl stood still on the stairs for a few minutes, then came running down and called out to her mother in an exaggeratedly cheerful tone. She did not want any breakfast yet, she said. "Going to take a little walk before I eat." Ducking out of the kitchen door, she melted into the woods and headed for the Secret Cove. It was absolutely necessary to be by herself for a while.

Bonnie'll have to wait a year. Bonnie'll have to wait a year. Those words followed her through the woods and across the swamp. They followed her to the moss-covered seat in Secret Cove. From there she could see a strip of blue and white morning sparkling in the sun. Everything sparkled out there today — the ripples in the water, the dazzling-white clouds, the sails of pleasure boats, the mica in the rocks; even the brown seaweed glistened. Yet there was no sparkle in Bonnie's eyes. For all she knew or cared, a thick curtain of fog might be hanging down in front of her.

Wait a year! Wait till the boys and girls of her own age had left her far behind! Wait till the people interested in her now had lost interest! Yet she couldn't possibly go to high school on the mainland without at least a few new clothes. She supposed she would have to write that nice Miss Bradley and give up the room at Broad Harbor.

What a summer! Just one thing after another had gone wrong. First, Ma's trip to the hospital. Then the *Anne Marie's* engine had had to go to the hospital too — that is to the repair shop — and that was an expensive business. To top all this the price of lobsters had dropped! There had been no chance for her to earn even a little money picking berries this summer, with all there had been to do at home.

She slumped down on the rock — a bundle of gloom.

Now laughing voices floated to her ears. They came from the old schooner right out of sailing-ship days which had anchored overnight just outside the inlet. The Windjammer Cruises were in full swing. How gay they sounded — those vacationers playing at sailing the *William Jenkins,* Camden, Maine, splashing into the sea for morning dips, sun-bathing, chattering. The schooner floated across the opening in the cove, off for an early start in the favoring breeze. Bonnie could see the red, green, blue, and pink spots made by the bright sweaters and sport shirts of the passengers. She was glad when they were gone out of her sight, out of her hearing.

Yet the laughter of those carefree creatures was still in her ears after the *William Jenkins* had gone out to sea. *They* didn't have to worry about money or sickness or anything else. *They* could pay nearly a hundred dollars for only a week's vacation! Yet for want of a hundred dollars her whole life was going to be changed, she thought bitterly. A hundred dollars would buy the things she absolutely had to have for school. It might just as well have been a thousand for all her chances of laying her hands on it. She glared at the sunlit world beyond the shady inlet as if she had a grudge against everything that was bright and gay anywhere.

Again a boat under full sail floated across the sunlit water. This was no old schooner, but a new one with shining hull and snowy sails. It was tall-masted, slender, graceful, like a beautiful sea bird that had floated out of the sky and alighted on the water for a moment.

A racing schooner this time! More rich summer folks. She would be glad when they were all gone — they and their expensive boats.

Ten or fifteen minutes later a twig snapped in the woods behind her. She sat up, scowling. Those twins! They had followed her over here. Why couldn't she ever be alone? The low-growing branches of the old spruce parted. A boy Bonnie had never seen before stepped out — a boy about her own age. One glance told her that he, too, was "summer folks." As Pa said, anybody who couldn't tell summer folks from islanders wouldn't know a salmon from a haddock. To be sure, this boy wore a T shirt and dungarees just as Jimmy and the other Bayberry boys did, but his haircut, his shoes, the redness of his sunburn and all sorts of little things stamped him as "not from around here." So did his voice when he called out, "Hi! I'm lost. How do I get to Bayberry Harbor?"

"Back that way and to the right." She pointed over her shoulder. "There's a path."

"Gosh! I sure did get turned around. And what a swamp I blundered into! Got in above my knees." He pointed to his dripping shoes and to his legs that were black with mud below his rolled-up dungarees.

"Where did you come from?" she asked bluntly.

"Off the *Summer Wind.*"

She laughed, thinking he put her off with a joke.

"That's a boat — the *Summer Wind* — my dad's boat. You can see it right out there." He pointed to the shining, tall-masted schooner. "We were on a cruise, but Mother's fallen hard for this island and wants to stay here. So I came ashore to scout around for a hotel and ended up here."

"There's Whalers' Inn at the Harbor," the girl vol-

unteered. "That's where all the summer folks stay —
all that come here. Not many come to Bayberry."

"You live on Bayberry?"

"Yes."

"All the year round?"

"Yes."

"Gosh! You're lucky. Live at the Harbor?"

Lucky! *He* thought *she* was lucky.

"No. Pretty Cove."

"Pretty Cove. Isn't that just where a pretty girl like
you would live! My name's Greg Watson — Greg for
Gregory — What's yours?"

"Bonnie Jean Andrews."

"Bonnie Jean from Pretty Cove. I'll sure remember
that. And you remember Greg Watson from Watson-
ville, Connecticut, will you? You might have me for
a neighbor yet. Mother says she wants a summer place
here and Mother's a great one to get what she wants."

He turned to leave, then caught sight of the minia-
ture village and exclaimed.

"Did you make that?" he wanted to know.

"My kid brothers and I did it together, with some
help from Jimmy Daniels. Jimmy works in a boatshop
and he got those models for us."

Andrews Village was quite complete now, with a
lighthouse, three cottages, a dock, a herring weir

and an assortment of boats moored in the harbor. The boy from Connecticut was obviously taken with it. "It's terrific," he told her. "Well, I've got to run before Mother gets worried. I'll be seeing you, Bonnie Jean." With a wave of his hand he was gone.

She stared at the place where the gay, good-looking boy had stood, then out through the inlet at the *Summer Wind,* half expecting that the shining boat and the boy had vanished at the same time. Neither seemed quite real, but more like a boy and a boat she had dreamed about while asleep on a summer morning. Yet the schooner was certainly real. It still rocked gently up and down out there with the tide, its sleek sides shinier than ever. Figures moved about on deck, figures in blue jackets and white caps.

How long had she been here? Bonnie asked herself suddenly. At least an hour! The sun hung noticeably higher than when she had slumped down here to think. Ma would wonder why she didn't come home and why she hadn't wanted any breakfast all this time. And Ma mustn't be worried, mustn't even know that her older daughter was upset. Reluctantly the girl left her seat by the quiet, make-believe village and went home.

6. Startling News

THE next afternoon Mr. Andrews came home bursting with a piece of news he had picked up at the Harbor. "Herb Thomas has gone and sold Cranberry Point — to *summer folks!* They're going to build a house out at the end of the Point."

His words stopped the whole family in their tracks. Cranberry Point sold! It was like having their own dooryard sold — and to perfect strangers. The Point was the place where they picked blueberries and cranberries and went fishing for flounder and pollock and watched the boats and waited for the *Anne Marie*.

"What's the name of the folks that bought it?" Bonnie asked suddenly.

"I forget. Somebody from Connecticut, seems to me."

"Was their name Watson?"

"That's it — Watson. How'd *you* know?"

"There was a boy over in the woods yesterday. He'd come ashore from a fancy schooner and got lost in the swamp. Said his name was Watson and he lived in Connecticut."

Not till next morning did Bonnie hear the worst. The Watsons had bought not only Cranberry Point but all the land — spruce woods, swamp, everything — from the edge of the Joyces' field to Johnson's pasture. They *owned* Secret Cove!

This news fell on her like a bombshell when she went to Mrs. Collins's store to buy a loaf of bread. "Guess you kids are going to miss playing over there in the little cove," remarked the storekeeper as she punched the cash register.

"But — but those folks haven't bought our —"

"They've bought every stick and stone 'tween Pretty Cove and the hill. Hey! Take your change."

Bonnie was dashing out of the door. She and the twins must get right over there and rescue their village before it was too late. Why did the Watsons have to buy all that land? Why did they have to buy that special place? She hated them.

"If they dare t-touch our v-village I'll, I'll . . . " stammered Dave when he heard the news, too excited to finish the threat.

"I'll set Chummy on them and he'll bite them just like he did that man that tried to steal Pa's dory," helped out Billy.

"Don't talk, boys. Just hurry." Bonnie knew that possession was nine tenths of the law. "Oh, dear, here comes Betty. I was hoping she didn't hear us."

The little girl came running and wailing, "Where the cap'ns and their little girls going to live now?"

Hot and out of breath they came to Secret Cove. Yanking aside the curtaining spruce branches, they peered down at Andrews Village. Everything was just as they had left it the day before. Bonnie let out a long sigh of relief. Now to get their boats and buildings out as quickly as possible. The boys pulled the little boats out of the water and Bonnie began stowing them in the clothesbasket, which they had brought along to carry them home in. Betty looked on and cried.

Startling News

The soft splash of oars sounded from the narrow entrance to the inlet. A rowboat was heading right in. A heavy-set man in slacks and a tweed jacket sat in the stern while a boy handled the boat.

"Hi, Bonnie Jean!"

The basket fell out of the girl's hands and splashed into the water, spilling out the boats. It was the Watson boy.

The rowboat inched its way through the shallow water and grounded noisily on the stony beach.

"Put everything back, *please*. I wanted Dad to see this place just the way you had it yesterday. This is my father. Dad, this is Bonnie Jean Andrews. She lives at Pretty Cove."

"It's ours," broke in Dave, while Chummy backed him up by growling deep down in his throat. "You can't . . ."

"Keep still, Dave! Shut up, Chummy!" ordered Bonnie.

"How do you do, Mr. Watson," she said to the man in the boat. "We know you've bought this land but we thought it would be all right to take our boats and things away. My brothers have worked hard here."

"Cap'n Hill and Cap'n Bailey and Cap'n Swan and their little girls live here," contributed Betty tearfully.

Bonnie explained about the imaginary population of the fishing village.

"They can keep right on living here, those little girls and their fathers," said the big man, smiling at Betty as he got out of the rowboat. "Greg thinks we should buy this little village and leave it here — that is, if you'll sell. Will you?"

"Sell!" repeated Bonnie, thinking she had not heard aright.

"Sell!" repeated the twins like bewildered echoes.

"I like you," said Betty. "I like you a bushel and a peck."

Mr. Watson turned to Bonnie. "How much will you take for this place just as it was before you began pulling it to pieces?"

"Why — why — " What *should* she say?

Billy saved her the trouble of deciding. "That village is worth real folding money. We won't take a cent less than ten dollars." His manner was amusingly imitative of men he had listened to as they bargained together.

Dave whistled under his breath. Where did Billy get the nerve to ask such a price as that?

Greg spoke up before his father could either accept or refuse Billy's ultimatum. "Dad, these kids don't know what this thing's worth. They've been working

50

on it since June, working hard, three of them. And some of their boats are models from a regular boat-shop over in Easton. Make them a *real* offer."

Mr. Watson stroked his plump cheek and thought for a few minutes as he picked up the boats and looked at them.

Five people stood still and waited. Bonnie held her breath.

"We-ell, how about a hundred dollars for the whole business?"

The twins burst out laughing.

Bonnie fixed her dark eyes on his face. *Was* he joking? There was not the slightest sign of anything but seriousness in his face. Yet he couldn't possibly be offering a hundred dollars for Andrews Village.

"Dad means that," said Greg.

"Gee!" Dave exploded. "Now you can go to high school sure, Bonnie."

So he had heard that conversation between Ma and Pa. Those twins never missed anything.

"And you and I can have those sweaters they've got over to the Harbor," planned Billy.

"I'll have a raincoat and a little umbrella like the little girl in the story." Betty was now putting in her claim. These two things had been her heart's greatest desires ever since Bonnie had read her about a girl who loved to go out in the rain because she had a red raincoat and a red umbrella.

Bonnie decided it was time to close the deal. This gold mine which had opened at her feet might close up again. "We'll take it, Mr. Watson."

"All right, young lady, you and the boys put everything back exactly the way Greg saw it the other day and I'll hand over the cash. And now to bind the bargain." He reached into his pocket, pulled out a billfold, extracted a ten-dollar bill and placed it on Bonnie's small, calloused palm. Her fingers closed over the crisp piece of paper.

"And now, skipper — " he turned to Greg as he spoke — "it's time we pushed off. We'll see you youngsters next week as soon as we're back from a little cruise on the *Summer Wind*."

None of the four spoke as they watched the rowboat being edged out between the rocks. Billy at last broke the silence. "You don't think he meant that about a hundred dollars, do you, Bonnie? *Do* you?"

"Why — I — don't — know." His sister seemed to be in a daze. "He acted like he did. And he's paid ten dollars down." She waved her fist with the bill clutched tightly in it; she was taking no chances of losing that bill.

They started for home on a run. They ran without

stopping across the swamp, through the woods, to burst into the kitchen. "Look, Ma — what we got — and — we're going — to . . ." Bonnie had to stop for breath. The twins were only too glad to take up the tale.

"Don't count on any more'n what you have," was Ma's advice. "That man's bound to change his mind about paying all that for a few toy boats and suchlike. But he can't take back the ten dollars."

Mrs. Joyce, when she heard about it, asked, "You kids got anything in writing? You ain't?" She shook her head pessimistically.

Mr. Andrews said Watson might or might not stick to his bargain. You never knew what summer folks would do or wouldn't do. "Anyhow, if he wants to throw his money around like that it's all right for you to take it." Like their mother, he seemed to think that only somebody not quite right in the head would offer a hundred dollars for a toy village.

In the afternoon the twins and Bonnie went back to Secret Cove to anchor the boats in the harbor again, set up the lighthouse and make everything shipshape.

Jimmy, when he came home as usual on Saturday, said the village was worth a hundred dollars. "Gee, Bonnie, it'll make all the difference about your going

53

to high school if that man does come across. Don't count on the money till you see it, though."

That evening she couldn't resist taking down one of the mail-order catalogues from the shelf in the living room and turning to *Junior Dresses,* then to *Junior Coats.* With the first tantalizing glimpse of the rows of pretty, smartly dressed girls pictured inside, she shut the book with an explosive slap of the pages and put it back quickly on the shelf. It just wouldn't do to spend that money, even in her imagination. The letdown would be too awful if she didn't get it.

7. A Perfect Day Ends

THE *Anne Marie* bobbed up and down impatiently on the tide in Pretty Cove. At least it seemed impatient to Bonnie because she herself was so eager to start. It was Sunday — a special Sunday. Every summer the Andrews family went to Long Island to see Aunt Grace and Uncle Bill and the six cousins. When the weather was fine there was always a lobster and corn roast on the beach. An outdoor feast seemed a certainty today. The only clouds in the sky were the puffy, cotton-wool variety. The breeze just rippled the surface of the sea.

Bonnie, the twins and Betty stood with the toes of their sneakers almost touching the water as they waited for Ma to stop thinking of one more thing, and still another, which somebody must go back to the house for and stow away in the clothesbasket, already heavily loaded with pies and cakes and jellies and pickles.

"Why can't we ever push off early?" grumbled Mr. Andrews when at last he had everybody and everything, including Chummy and the big basket, packed into the dory and was rowing out to the *Anne Marie*. A beautiful quiet fell on grown folks, young folks and dog when he started the engine. Only Betty talked and she spoke softly to the doll in her lap. None of them were ever bored or impatient on the water.

It seemed to Bonnie that boat engines always hummed more musically on Sundays than on weekdays and that lobster boats skipped along with a friskiness never seen on working days. All craft putting out from the island were pleasure craft today. Lobster buckets, nets, tuna spears — the paraphernalia of weekday life — had been left behind. In their place small, bobbing heads rose above gunwales, and the figures of stout women. Some boatloads were going fishing for fun. Others like the *Anne Marie's* were going visiting. Still others were just "going places."

Bonnie watched for a certain long ridge of dark blue to rise against the sky beyond the smaller, nearer islands. Then she watched for it to lengthen and turn from blue to green. That was Long Island. Then she watched for a white spot. That was the beach at Windham's Cove. Now six pairs of eyes were focused on that same spot. The beach grew larger. Rocks loomed up on it and the figures of people could be distinguished moving about against the white sand.

"They're there!"

"All of them."

"That's Uncle Billy waving his cap, and Aunt Grace waving her apron."

"There's the baby on a blanket."

"Look! They've got dinner cooking."

"Yoo-hoo. Yoo-hoo."

"Hi, everybody."

The *Anne Marie* dropped anchor.

On the beach, in addition to seven people of various ages and a baby, was a large, round, built-up place that looked like a large brown flower bed. From it issued mouth-watering smells. Lobsters, clams and ears of corn roasted and steamed there under a blanket of seaweed. Uncle Billy and the older boys had cut short their Sunday naps to lay a bed of stones and build a great fire on top of them. When the stones were red-hot, the men had raked off the coals and embers, laid lobsters, clams and corn in layers on the stones, and covered everything with a thick blanket of wet seaweed.

"Smells ready t'eat and fit t'eat too," remarked Pa, with his usual brevity.

The two girls, the twins and Chummy all sniffed like hounds taking up a scent. There wasn't any other smell so delicious as lobsters, clams and corn all steaming together and seasoned with seaweed.

Now began the ceremony of lifting the seaweed and uncovering the dinner. A cloud of fragrant steam arose. The dinner was ready to eat.

They sat on the rocks and ate till the mound of lobsters, clams and corn had been reduced to shells, claws and thoroughly gnawed ears, and the pie plates stared emptily up from the ground. They ate till no one, including Chummy, could swallow even one mouthful more. Then the young people played around on the beach and clambered over the rocks, and fished off the rocks for pollock and flounder, while the grown folks exchanged the accumulated family news of months.

A *Perfect Day Ends*

"Why don't we have lobster roasts every Sunday?" asked Betty on the way home.

"Every Sunday!" exclaimed her mother. "We'd be dead if we stuffed like that more'n once a year."

At sunset the *Anne Marie* came humming back into Pretty Cove with a load of happy people. As Pa dropped anchor, Chummy ran to the prow of the boat and began to bark at someone who seemed to be waiting onshore for the family. It was Mabel Collins, perched on a rock like one of the crows that were still picking about for shellfish and bits of refuse. Mabel sat still and watched the dory as Pa rowed in. Even before the rowboat grated on the beach she was announcing her news.

"Some boys come in a little boat from somewheres and they went into Secret Cove and after they was gone I went right over there and they'd took your little boats and knocked things to pieces there and —"

At this point Betty burst into a loud wail, drowning out anything more Mabel might have to say. Bonnie took a firm hold of Mabel's arm and fixed her with a searching look.

"Are you telling us the truth? *Are* you, Mabel?"

"Cross my heart and hope to die. If you don't believe me go over there and look for yourself." She ended as usual with that maddening giggle of hers.

They went — all four of them. They dived out of the rosy light that flooded Pretty Cove into the dusky woods. They leaped from hummock to hummock across the swamp. They pelted through the woods beyond the swamp. Four hearts thumped hard as Billy, who was ahead, pulled the branches of the spruce aside. The others peered over and around him at the pool. All the bright color drained out of Bonnie's face. For once, at least, Mabel had told the truth. Andrews Village lay in ruins — the lighthouse toppled over, the weir broken. All the best of the boats were gone.

8. Andrews Village in Ruins

JUST let me get hold of those guys," Billy raged.
"I'll show the dirty bums," threatened Dave,
squaring off at an imaginary enemy. "I'll make them
give us back our boats."

Betty could not say what she would do for crying.

Bonnie was silent and deeply thoughtful as they
hurried back through the fast-darkening woods. She
realized quite suddenly how much she had counted
on Mr. Watson and the rest of that hundred dollars.

Now they would even have to return his crisp, beautiful ten-dollar bill.

"Maybe," she suggested on a sudden small wave of hope, "they didn't take the boats away. Maybe they hid them somewhere. We'll go back in the morning when there's more light and we'll look in among the rocks."

She didn't feel particularly confident, but her words at least had the effect of quieting the almost hysterical children.

Early next morning, without stopping for a bite of breakfast, the four of them plunged through the woods again. This time they searched Secret Cove with the thoroughness of a bunch of detectives — under overhanging rocks, in every small niche between rocks, in among the roots of trees. They examined the pebbly beach for footprints and marks of a boat's prow and for any small article that might have been dropped there. Unfortunately it was the time of a full moon and the tide had been extra high the night before. There was no clue to the identity of the mysterious boys.

Nobody but Mabel had seen them. Her description of the rowboat and its crew of light-haired boys, in dungarees and with fishlines, could fit anybody. Both the Joyces and the McAdams had been away all day, not returning till after the Andrews family. Mrs. Collins had not been out of her house and from where she lived there was no view of Pretty Cove or the Point. The unreliable Mabel remained the only witness.

Had Mabel herself gone berserk over in Secret Cove, Bonnie wondered, and then made up a story about boys in a boat? Mabel had been known to fly into a temper and smash things right and left. Yet there seemed no reason for her to get mad in Secret Cove. And wouldn't the foolish girl have given herself away by now? Would she have been smart enough to hide all those boats where no one, not even her mother, could discover them?

"Well, we've got to straighten the place out anyhow," Bonnie told the twins. "Perhaps Mr. Watson'll let us keep the ten dollars if we do that."

They went to work next morning, setting up the lighthouse again, which had been left tumbled over, half in the water and half out, rebuilding tipped-over houses, making new masts for the three boats which had been knocked about but not carried off by the vandals, mending the broken weir. By the end of another day only those empty spaces where boats had been moored told of the sack of Andrews Village.

"If we just had time to get some more boats. If we

just *had!*" said Bonnie, staring down at the once crowded little harbor.

"We can whittle out another sailboat — Dave and me," suggested Billy.

"Maybe Pa could make us a lobster boat," added Billy.

Still the prize boats — the model boats — would be missing. Then Bonnie had an idea. "I'll write to Jimmy," she told herself, "and see if he can help us."

The letter — a long one — was addressed to Mr. James Daniels, care of Murphy's Boatshop, Easton, Maine. In it Bonnie told the sad mystery story of what had happened in Secret Cove. . . .

. . . We're in a terrible spot because we agreed that by the time the Watsons got back we'd have everything just as it was when Greg first saw Andrews Village. His Dad certainly won't think it's worth a hundred dollars now. Guess we'll be lucky if he doesn't want his ten dollars back.

Was there any chance, Bonnie asked him, of getting some more models from the shop? She could pay Mr. Murphy ten dollars. Those boats would make all the difference between her going to school or not going to school in September.

Bonnie did not mention the letter to the twins or to

anyone else. Every morning she ran out on the Point and looked anxiously over to Bayberry Harbor, where the *Summer Wind* was usually moored, to make sure the Watsons were still away. Every afternoon she went to the post office as soon as the mail boat arrived and waited while the mail was sorted out.

Saturday came. Still no reply from Jimmy. Early that morning, before Bonnie had a chance to run out on the Point, Mabel Collins brought the news that "them folks with the fancy boat is back." Bonnie, who never believed a word the girl said until she verified it, dashed out to the end of Cranberry Point to see for herself. Yes, there lay the *Summer Wind* at the mooring in Bayberry Harbor.

"Hurry, boys," she told the twins, "bring that sailboat you've made, even if you didn't get it painted, and the lobster boat Pa whittled out. They'll fill up some space. Then I'll go over to the hotel and tell those people just what happened and what we've done about it."

Dave tied the sail onto the schooner as he went. Billy produced a replica of the *Anne Marie* which was complete except for a mast. The three started out.

At the edge of the woods they heard splashing sounds coming from Secret Cove. That Watson boy!

65

Why *couldn't* he have waited ten minutes? That would have been time enough to anchor the new boats in the water.

"Gosh! What'd you kids come so early for? Wanted to surprise you." A light-haired boy in overalls squatted by the pool. It was Jimmy! He was just sliding the last of four shiny new boats into the harbor of Andrews Village.

"Boy! They're sharp. They're sharp," chorused the twins, jumping up and down.

"They're even nicer than the others. Did they cost more than ten dollars?" Bonnie's voice grew suddenly anxious.

"Won't cost you a cent. I showed the boss your letter and told him how if you didn't get some more boats right off you'd lose a hundred dollars. He got busy and dug these up and I dusted them off and painted them. And if that man doesn't come across now with the rest of the money, he's a cheat and I'll tell him so."

"Oh Jimmy! You're simply the most . . . " Bonnie never got a chance to finish.

"Skip it!" interrupted embarrassed Jimmy. "I didn't do a thing but show Fred Murphy your letter."

❋   ❋   ❋

"Boy! Did you ever see such a lot of folding money?" whispered Dave.

"Not me!" whispered back Billy.

It was Monday. The place was Secret Cove. The sale of Andrews Village had just been completed. The boys were watching Mr. Watson as he peeled from a sizable wad five twenty-dollar bills and counted them out onto Bonnie's palm.

"That's ten dollars too much," she told him. "You paid us ten last week."

"I know. But I've been hearing about all the trouble you kids have had since then. You've earned another ten all right."

"Why — why — thank you, sir."

Greg stood looking on with the air of having managed the deal. "Will this really make a difference about your going to school, Bonnie Jean?"

"Just all the difference," said the girl gravely. It was nice of this boy, she thought, to be so interested when he hardly knew her at all.

They blew out of the woods and into the house like a September gale. Ma had to take the money in her hands and count it before she believed they actually had a hundred dollars. She still had some doubts, too, about it being right to take so much money for just a toy village. "Still, your Pa's always saying that summer folks like to throw money around. It makes them feel good. So I guess you may's well keep it." She headed straight for the mail-order catalogues and laid the two heavy volumes on the kitchen table, where they could all look at them together. Quickly five chairs were pulled up to the table. Quickly five heads bent over the books. It was hard to tell which one was the most excited as they turned the alluring pages.

It was a bewildering and time-consuming business for Bonnie — to pick out so many things at once. All sorts of choices were involved.

"How do you like this coat?" Mrs. Andrews would ask, only to add, "I'm afraid that wouldn't be warm enough."

Again Bonnie would pick out a model, and discover that it came only in blue and green. Hers just had to be red or brown.

The twins had problems, too. Having decided to order their sweaters instead of buying at the Harbor store, they were faced with difficult choices between sweaters with moose on the front and sweaters with ducks flying across them, between red sweaters and blue sweaters.

Betty was the only one who knew exactly what she wanted and turned to the right page at once. Weeks ago she had put a slip of paper in the catalogue, after Bonnie had found for her that page full of pictures of little girls in raincoats.

Of course the money did not buy anything like as many things as they had expected. "You'll have to use my old suitcase," Ma said, after they had gone through the pages of suitcases, traveling bags and hatboxes in both catalogues. "We can get the strap mended and put a little shoe polish on those worn places." Two pairs of shoes were cut down to one. A rayon-and-wool skirt was substituted for an all-wool skirt. Bonnie's nighties and slips would *all* have to be homemade, though she longed for just one of those dainty, lacy ones in the catalogue. However, her brown coat lined with red and the gay print dress for festive occasions were prettier than any clothes she had ever possessed in her life. And she was going to have a pair of red shoes!

When the order was at last filled out, Bonnie took it to the Harbor post office and sang all the way. Coming back over the hill, she noticed that stakes had already been driven into the ground out on the Point. That was where the new house would go up, she supposed. Looked as if they planned to build a big one, too. Once that was built, everything was going to seem different at Pretty Cove — no mistake about that. "We shan't fence anything in," Greg's father had said this morning. "You youngsters can come over here to the little cove any time you want to, and out on the Point."

Yet nothing he could say would ever make Secret Cove their special place again. And by another summer Cranberry Point would be the Watson's dooryard instead of a fishing and berry-picking place for anyone who wanted to go there, and especially for Pretty Cove.

However, Bonnie had little time during those next few weeks to think of Cranberry Point or of much of anything except her own plans for her immediate future. Next summer was a long way off.

9. All Aboard for Sanford

ON the day after Labor Day the mail boat from
Bayberry Harbor carried a heavy cargo.
Suitcases, hatboxes, duffel bags, cartons, were piled
high wherever they could be set down, propped up
or tied on. Passengers filled deck seats and cabin
seats. They sat on their luggage and stood up. Two
schoolteachers from Boston, who owned a cottage at
Goose Cove, the couple who ran the Lobster Pot, a
tearoom at the Harbor, a number of guests from
Whalers' Inn and the college boys and girls who had

been working there this summer — all these were aboard.

Two island girls and an island boy were also on board. The plump, brown-haired girl was Mary Lunt. The light-haired boy was Jimmy. The girl who looked like a red-and-brown autumn leaf and couldn't keep still a minute was Bonnie Jean Andrews. She was wearing her new outfit — brown coat with red lining, brown skirt, red sweater, topped by a red beanie. From her arm swung the beautiful red handbag. Her cheeks were as red as the beanie. She sat down only to jump right up again, climbed up and down the ladder to the dock twice in ten minutes, and didn't stop talking at all.

"Relax, Bonnie," Jimmy told her.

"You sure do get excited," laughed Mary, who wouldn't have acted excited if the boat were on fire.

It was all right for those two to talk, thought the girl from Pretty Cove. For Jimmy this was an old story. As for Mary, she was going to live with a cousin in Bellport, where she had visited often. Suppose *she* was going to a place where she didn't know a soul. Suppose *she* was going to live with strangers and baby-sit with kids she'd never even seen, kids who might turn out to be awful brats. Perhaps even the placid Mary might feel excited in a case like that.

72

All Aboard for Sanford

Everything had happened so fast since that day a hundred and ten dollars fell out of the sky. All sorts of preparations had had to be made quickly. The new skirts needed hemming up, the old ones letting down. There were the nightgowns and slips to be made and the red sweater to be finished. Then came an orgy of washing and home dry cleaning and packing. Bonnie and her mother had filled the old suitcase till its worn sides bulged, then wrapped up the overflow and sent it parcel post to — Miss Bonnie Jean Andrews, 24 Pine Street, Broad Harbor, Maine. How queer that address looked!

"Now Bonnie," called her mother as the girl was heading for the ladder again, "you stay on the boat. Cap'n Taylor'll be casting off any moment now."

"All aboar-r-rd," rolled out the captain. It was too late for any more last messages. The boy on the dock tossed over the rope. The boat was cut loose from Bayberry Island, and so was Bonnie.

"Good-by!" "Good-by!" "Good-by!" "Good-by!" shouted four voices.

"Good-by Ma. Good-by Dave. Good-by Billy. Good-by Betty."

"Don't forget to . . . " The engine's roar drowned out the rest of her mother's reminder to write. It also drowned out the hysterical barking of Chummy, who

73

had to be forcibly restrained from leaping into the departing boat.

Bonnie waved till the people on the dock looked no bigger than dolls, till they couldn't possibly tell whether she waved or not. When her family had melted into the dark background of the dock, the red and brown figure was suddenly very still. Settling down in front of the pilothouse with Mary and Jimmy, among luggage and freight, she fixed her eyes straight ahead on the strip of mainland that rose out there from behind the islands. For a long time she did not say a word.

A whistle blew loudly from starboard. A tall-masted schooner under full sail and under power as well cut swiftly through the water and overtook the mail boat. The shining prow bore the name *Summer Wind.* The passengers on both boats waved. A boy on the *Summer Wind's* deck turned a pair of binoculars on the other craft, then shouted, "Good-by Bonnie Jean! Good luck!"

"He's a fresh guy — that Watson boy!" exclaimed Jimmy. "And I don't care much for his boat either, with all its speed."

"Fresh guy or not, I wouldn't be going to school right now if it hadn't been for him. It was all his idea that his father should buy Andrews Village."

74

"You'd have found some other way." Jimmy evidently did not want to give any credit to the newcomers. "Anyway, they probably bought your village just to show off. Gee! I wish folks wouldn't sell any more land to summer folks. Pretty soon we'll all have to move off Bayberry and let them have it, just like the folks on Seal Island."

Bonnie said nothing. She felt like standing up for "that Watson boy," but was in no mood to argue with Jimmy — not now, when everything familiar was sinking out of sight faster and faster behind her.

She began to feel frighteningly on her own — cut loose in a new world. More and more the girl wondered what Mrs. Barnes would be like, Mrs. Barnes of 24 Pine Street, with whom Bonnie was going to live for nearly a year. Each of them had taken the other sight unseen on the word of Miss Bradley from the Sea Coast Mission.

Up to now, Bonnie had been too busy to wonder much about this stranger. But as the miles between her and Pine Street lessened, her imagination grew active. Suppose they didn't like each other — she and this "nice person for Bonnie to live with"! Would she be fussy? Would she understand girls? To be sure, Mrs. Barnes had a daughter, but a four-year-old was awfully different from a fourteen-year-old. So few people seemed to understand how a girl in her teens felt! Ma did, but she was different. Better stop thinking about Ma — and home.

The boat put in to Spring Harbor — the first stop on the mainland. "Good-by Bonnie. Good luck," said Mary, gathering up her bags and bundles. This was where she took the train for Bellport.

"You're next," Bonnie solemnly reminded Jimmy. After Jimmy got off to take the Easton bus, she would be entirely cut loose from Bayberry. Wings fluttered in her stomach.

"I'm going on to Broad Harbor and see you get there O.K. There's a bus I can take back to Easton from there."

"Oh, Jimmy!" She could have thrown her arms right around his neck, but one didn't do things like that to a boy as reserved as Jimmy.

"That's O.K. I've got all day."

Bonnie sat back and relaxed for the first time since five o'clock that morning.

Contentedly she munched half the chocolate bar she had brought, while the boy ate the other half. Then they shared the apple he pulled out of his pocket.

In about an hour they could see Broad Harbor like a toy village out beyond the harbors and coves that scalloped the shore. It grew into a good-sized town with spires and high buildings sticking up above the houses, with paved streets running up from what seemed to the girl an enormous dock, with a harbor crowded with boats. Only once before had she been here and that was a number of years ago. The Andrews family had neither time nor need for trips to town nor money to pay for them. Most of their friends and relatives lived on Bayberry or on neighboring islands. Most of their shopping was done by mail.

What a difference it made to have Jimmy along! He had worked here one summer. He knew just where Pine Street was and helped her to find the number. Shy though he was, he even introduced himself and Bonnie to the young woman who opened the door.

"Come right in," said Mrs. Barnes.

"Good-by," said the boy quickly, as soon as Bonnie's suitcase was deposited in the hall. Then he whispered, "Keep your chin up. Don't let anybody in Broad Harbor know you feel like a lost puppy."

How did Jimmy know that was exactly how she *did* feel?

He was off.

"Perhaps you'd like to see your room and unpack

77

a bit," suggested Mrs. Barnes. She was younger and prettier than Bonnie had pictured her. She didn't look at all like a fussy person. She might even understand girls in their teens a little, Bonnie decided, when she saw the small upstairs room that was to be hers. It had a couch instead of a bed and there were bright cushions on it. There were curtains the color of sunshine at the windows. The low table was just the right height for studying and writing.

It was a very pretty room, much prettier than her room at home, with more furniture. Yet it seemed empty. Two things were lacking. She missed them especially after she went to bed that night. One was the familiar *swish-swash* of the water in the Cove. The other was a little brown-haired girl asleep beside her with a dirty rag doll in her arms.

10. Bonnie Keeps Her Chin Up

E VER been in Broad Harbor before?"
"Of course I have."

Norma, the girl who lived at number 22 Pine Street, raised her beautifully shaped eyebrows. She had decided on this first day of school to take the "cute little island girl" next door under her wing. They were walking out Main Street together.

"A girl in my class — I'm a sophomore, you know — comes from Black Island and until last year she'd never been on the mainland at all. She'd never used a telephone, never turned on an electric light. Imagine that!"

The island girl's chin shot upward. "You ever been on Black Island?"

"Why, no. Why should I?"

"Ever been on Seal? . . . On Bayberry? . . . On Long?"

The sophomore shook her pretty blond head as the questions were pelted at her.

"Ever been out in a seiner and seen them scoop up herring? . . . Ever seen anybody spear a whopping big tuna?"

The answer was still no.

"Imagine that!" Bonnie mimicked the other's voice and superior air perfectly.

The two walked along in complete silence. Presently Bonnie stopped and made up a wholly imaginary errand. "Forgot something I have to get at the store. Don't wait." One thing she would not do — arrive on this first morning at a strange school with a girl who patronized her.

"Of all the queers! That's the last time I'll be nice to her," said Norma.

Bonnie walked to school by herself, and with her chin tilted at an entirely unnatural angle. She had never before felt quite so alone.

Bonnie Keeps Her Chin Up

There seemed to be thousands of boys and girls in and around the long, two-story building when she arrived. They chattered in bunches, like starlings. They kicked footballs and bounced basketballs. They crowded in and out of the front hall. Everybody seemed to know everybody else. "Hi, Red!" "Hi, Nancy!" "Hi, Jane!" "Hi, Doug!" The "Hi's" spattered like a shower around her as she walked self-consciously across the yard and up the crowded steps. Yet no one said, "Hi, Bonnie." There must have been other girls there who felt strange, but the Bayberry Island girl didn't see them. All she saw was one big, happy reunion.

Bonnie tried hard to act as if she knew her way about, first pretending to be in a tremendous hurry and dashing up the steps and into the hallway, then rushing to the drinking fountain as if she couldn't bother with anybody until she got a drink of water. Since she wasn't used to a drinking fountain, more of the water landed on her sweater than in her mouth. Buttoning up her coat to cover the spatters, she sauntered in what she thought was a bored manner up and down the hall. The attempt evidently failed. Anyway, a tall boy with a B on the front of his pullover, who came by just then, grinned and sang out, "Cheer up, little girl. You'll get used to us."

81

She laughed for the first time in nearly twenty-four hours.

"What's your name?"

Before she could tell him there was a chorus of "Hi, Tom," and a bunch of boys and girls closed in on him.

Now Bonnie stood at a window and acted as though she were watching for someone.

"Oh, here you are!" called a voice to her back. She whirled around.

"Excuse me. I thought you were Anne," said the girl, looking disappointed.

It was a relief when a bell clanged and ended all this sociability-for-everybody-but-her. She followed the others wherever they all seemed to be going.

The whole day was not like its beginning nor were all the girls like Norma. There were friendly girls and helpful girls. There were other girls as lonely and scared as she. And there was Susan Miller. Susan was fair-haired and sweet-faced and came from Woods Island. She had heard that a girl from Bayberry Island was a freshman too and lost no time in finding her.

"We're practically neighbors," said Bonnie when the other island girl introduced herself. There and then the two joined forces. They gave each other confidence through that first confusing day of learning the ropes in a school with eight teachers instead of one and fifteen times as many boys and girls as either had even seen at one time. And they liked each other "a bushel and a peck," as Betty would have put it.

At the end of the day the two walked home together with arms interlocked and heads close together, comparing experiences. They were agreed about everything — that they felt almost dizzy, that they got all turned around in that big schoolhouse, that some of the teachers scared them to death and that this one or that one was nice, almost as nice as Miss Smith or Miss Brown at home.

Then there were all those extra things to talk about — the school chorus, the school band, dramatics, the teams. Bonnie wanted to be in the chorus and to act in plays and perhaps play basketball. Susan wasn't sure about the other things but she would like to learn to play basketball. They agreed that all this business of "trying out" for things sounded terrifying.

"And we've got to make some sense out of *these*," groaned Susan.

"These" were an algebra book and a first-year Latin.

"We'll do just as well as the rest," the girl from

Bayberry Island insisted. "They've never had algebra or Latin before either. And keep your chin up, Susan."

As for her own chin, it fairly ached from being kept up. She was glad to be alone in her own little room where she could relax that small, determined chin. How good it was to get away from all those strange faces that looked at you and seemed to say, "Who are you and where'd you come from?" There were no unfamiliar faces on her island. Everybody — young, old and middle-aged — knew everybody else, except for a couple of months in summer when there were summer folks at the inn and at a few cottages. Tonight she'd be glad to see just anybody from Bayberry Island — even Mabel Collins.

Bonnie had little time to be lonely or homesick until Saturday. Then came the first week end, also the first baby-sitting. Mr. and Mrs. Barnes went out Saturday evening. She got along swimmingly with the two children after all her experience with youngsters. The bad part was being alone in a strange house. When the last drink of water had been brought and the last good night said, she suddenly became aware of all sorts of queer sounds. Were those footsteps on the porch? What made the stairs creak like that? Was somebody prowling about in the yard? She longed for the snug house at Pretty Cove, where the little sounds were all familiar, harmless sounds and the sea swished softly almost at her doorstep.

Sunday was worse than Saturday. Most of the time she was not in Broad Harbor at all. That is, her thoughts were over in Pretty Cove. In imagination she followed the Andrews family through the day from hour to hour. What were they doing now? Eating breakfast? Were Ma and Pa and the kids at this minute walking across Cranberry Point and up the hill to the white-spired church that looked down on Bayberry Harbor? Was Pa cleaning up the *Anne Marie* for an afternoon trip? What was Ma cooking for dinner? Corn hake? Yummy! She could smell the fish and potatoes cooking together.

The Barneses invited her to dinner. They had roast chicken and ice cream. It somehow didn't taste good.

Bonnie was actually glad to hear her alarm clock jangling on Monday morning. Her first Sunday was behind her. She felt like a new recruit who has just come through his first battle. Nothing, no matter what happened, would ever seem quite so hard again. Week after next her father would come on Friday night and take her home for over Sunday. That week end was seven days nearer now.

Pa came just as he had promised. He arrived at

dusk from the round of his lobster traps. At sight of him coming up the steps of number 24 in khaki pants and faded sweater, wearing his battered, stained felt hat, a door seemed to open for the girl back into the world of Bayberry Island.

Down at Broad Harbor dock the *Anne Marie* bobbed up and down, her port and starboard lights gleaming like red and green jewels. Confidently she nosed her way out of the island-strewn harbor into the channel, her searchlight opening a bright path ahead. You couldn't faze the *Anne Marie* with islands. Now they were out in the channel, cutting through black water under stars so clear and big they looked artificial.

After a while she began to watch for landmarks. That long, humpy mass along the horizon was Long Island. Now Black Island poked its dark nose from behind Long Island and behind that rose the bare rocks of Gull Island. Next came Goose Island and finally Seal Island, all notched by the pointed tops of trees. Then a dark, sharp point — Cranberry Point! Bayberry Harbor Light winked at her. She was home. She could name the places alongshore. The house where the windows were yellow upstairs and down was the Campbell house; two families lived there. The one with a light over the front door was Captain

Otis's. He always hung a lantern there. And so on.

Pa began calling to the boats they met, boats starting out from Bayberry for a night of fishing. He knew them all. Bonnie recognized many of those voices calling back so cheerfully across the water.

He gave the wheel a quick swing. They were heading out to clear the long tail of Cranberry Point. The whole of Pretty Cove was waiting to call "Hi, Bonnie!" and "Welcome home, Bonnie." The twins and Betty and Ma stood on the beach. The twins held Chummy by the collar to keep him from swimming out. Children and dog were all ready to pounce on her the instant she stepped from the dory. "Don't smother her," warned Ma. "Let her get out. Keep holding onto Chummy."

It was as if she had never been away. Broad Harbor, Broad Harbor High School, the Barnes family, the teachers, even Susan — all had been left back in that other world.

On Sunday afternoon, when she set out again, Bonnie found that saying good-by was not quite so hard this time. Leaving home would never again be the wrench it had been in September.

11. The Hardest Test

M ISS Bell's glasses looked like a microscope focused on a specimen, with Bonnie as the specimen. The senior girl and the junior boy who sat flanking the English teacher seemed more like courtroom judges than schoolmates. "Don't stare at me like that," she wanted to say. Why had she ever let herself in for this anyway?

Bonnie was trying out for a part in the school play, not only for a part but for the lead. "Pamela Allen, a spoiled, sophisticated girl who talks and sings in a throaty voice" — this was the role bright-eyed, unsophisticated Bonnie Jean from Bayberry Island had picked for herself.

It seemed for a moment that her voice was gone. She managed somehow to scrape the hoarseness down and to begin, "I'm bored, bored with everything and everybody," looking scared and excited but certainly not bored.

"And now," said Miss Bell, "try the song in Act II."

> The moon is lo-ow
> The night is o-old —

Where was that throaty voice Bonnie had been practicing in her room for days? This voice coming out of her mouth was thin, sweet and a little tremulous.

> And you are gone
> And what care I-I-I?

Gosh, how that last note quavered! Pamela, the sophisticated Pamela, would never sing like that.

"Thank you," said Miss Bell.

Bonnie had only one idea — to get out of the room as quickly as possible. The teacher's voice halted her on the way to the door.

"How about trying one of the other parts now?"

The girl shook her head vigorously. "Pamela's is

the only one I even read over." She had, as a matter of fact, practically memorized Pamela.

"Why not try just a few lines of Ellen's part?" added the senior persuasively. "Ellen's quite important. She straightens everything out at the end."

Bonnie glanced down at the cast of characters and read, *Ellen — Pamela's cousin, a quiet girl who says little but thinks a lot.*

Who would want to take a mousy part like that? Yet with those three looking at her expectantly she felt compelled. Without half trying, she read off a few lines and almost ran from the room, then went dashing out of the building, out of the schoolyard, past Susan and the other boys and girls as if in too much of a hurry to speak to anybody.

"How did it go, Bonnie?" called Susan.

"Tell you later."

In the quiet of her own room at number 24, she kicked herself vigorously for being so scared, raged at the idea of even considering acting the girl who "says little but thinks a lot," and vowed she'd refuse such a consolation prize if anybody offered it to her. She finally calmed down enough to tackle the algebra assignment. Yet the fires that had flamed up in her cheeks during the tryout did not die down for an hour.

Next morning the crowd was six deep around the school bulletin board, where the cast of the play was posted. Bonnie couldn't get near it. She didn't need to. "You're in the play!" one after another called at sight of her. "Oh, Bonnie, I'm so glad," cried Susan, throwing her arms around her.

"What part did I get?" The question was answered before she finished asking it. All around her ecstatic voices cried out, congratulating someone else.

"Oh, Norma, you've got the lead!"

"You'll be terrific as Pamela."

"That's wonderful, Norma."

Well that did it! Never would she play second to Norma's leading lady. Not she!

"Hadn't you better take a little time to think it over?" asked Miss Bell, looking into the island girl's hot, unhappy face. "It's a real honor to be in a school play, especially in your first year."

"I just can't do that part," repeated Bonnie for the third time.

The woman behind the desk looked so disappointed in her that Bonnie decided to blurt out the truth. "Miss Bell, I couldn't possibly act with Norma. She'd — she'd put me all out." Bonnie couldn't tell the *whole* truth — that this sophomore, from the first

91

day of school, had never missed a chance to be disagreeably patronizing to "the little island girl." She always referred to her thus.

"Norma can't put you out if you have enough respect for yourself."

Bonnie recalled what Jimmy had said — that he had had to show the boys at Easton High that he knew his way around. Well, she would *show* Norma.

"I'll do it, Miss Bell." She went out of the room with her chin leading.

It was one thing to say she'd show Norma and another thing to do it at rehearsals. Bonnie would learn her lines perfectly. Then Norma would fix those cold blue eyes on her and the words would come out falteringly. In the next few weeks Bonnie discovered how many subtle tricks a leading lady can use to fluster another player. A sidelong glance noticed only by herself said, "Bet you don't know that line." A slight change in a cue or an impatient gesture or a question — "Miss Bell, don't you think Ellen would say that line in a stage whisper?" or "Wouldn't Ellen walk on stage more slowly?" In all these ways Norma tried to confuse her.

Bonnie came out of the rehearsals biting her lower lip and holding back tears. Once she decided to give up the part. Then she made a discovery that stiffened her spine into an iron rod. "Do you know why Norma is acting that way?" Susan asked one day.

"Because she hates me."

"Partly. But she's got another reason. She wanted her girl friend Freda to get Ellen's part. I heard her say so. And she thinks she can make you quit or get yourself dropped."

After that Bonnie would have walked through a curtain of fire to play Ellen. This was a test just as much as a classroom test. Jimmy had had to pass his with his fists. She had to pass hers by proving that she could play Ellen to Norma's Pamela, play under the enemy's guns.

The Christmas vacation drew near. Susan marked off the days left before its beginning one by one on her calendar. Bonnie tried not to notice how fast time ticked away. Susan sang, "I'm dreaming of a white Christmas." Bonnie did not sing at all. For her the approaching holiday brought nearer and nearer an awful night — the night the play would be performed.

What might not Norma do that night? Change the cues? Trip her up somehow without seeming to? She had heard of actors and actresses doing awful things out of spite. And Norma was full of spite. No doubt about that. There was a nasty gleam in the sophomore's eyes at rehearsals now. There was a large flock of butterflies in the freshman's stomach.

To make things harder, not a soul from Bayberry Island would be in the audience — nobody who believed in her and really knew what she could do. Ma and Pa would not be there looking happy and expectant, or Jimmy, grinning his confidence that she would come through.

The night of the dress rehearsal came. Norma, smartly gotten up, Norma with mascaraed eyes, looked more than ever to Bonnie like nothing human. She was supposed to be a disdainful lady in the play and she acted the part to the hilt. As for herself, Bonnie knew, without looking at Miss Bell, that she had been a washout.

On the great night there were no butterflies in the island girl's stomach. A cold stone had taken their place. There was also a lump in her throat, which stayed there no matter how much she swallowed, and she felt so queasy it seemed absurd to try to go on at all.

All made up and ready, she stood and clung to a post for support and peeked out from the wing to watch the hall fill. Everybody in school was there, including all the teachers. The families and friends of the performers had come — but not her family, not her friends. Not much like a Bayberry Harbor Town Hall audience!

Wait a minute! A tall, lanky boy had just come in, a boy with light hair, lots of freckles and blue eyes. It was Jimmy! Jimmy, come all the way from Easton to see her in the play!

The curtain went up. Bonnie found that she could walk onto the stage even though her legs felt as if she had had the flu. Norma, who was seated on the stage, had the first line. But where was the self-possessed girl of rehearsals? Stark terror stared out of the mascara. The hand reached out to Cousin Ellen in greeting was a piece of ice. An awful silence followed — a silence that seemed to Bonnie a half hour long. Now she saw frantic appeal in the glassy eyes.

In desperation Bonnie squeezed Norma's cold hand and made up some lines to give the leading lady time to pull herself together. In a few moments, to Bonnie's inexpressible relief, the sophomore snapped out of her stage fright and was herself again. No, not quite herself, not the Lady Disdainful of rehearsals, someone more human.

At the end of the act, Miss Bell waited backstage, waited to smile and say, "Bonnie, I'm proud of you. You're a real trouper." She had seen just what had happened at the beginning of the play.

Susan was there, too, to hug her and say, "Bonnie, you were wonderful."

Jimmy grinned clear across his face when she came back and spoke to him. He was pleased with her and pleased with himself for having sprung a surprise on her.

"You're terrific. Just keep it up. Won't be seeing you at the end. Have to cut and run as soon as it's over or I'll miss my bus. See you next week on the mail boat."

"I'm dreaming of a white Christmas," sang Bonnie next day, with a gay lilt in her voice. She did not care whether it was white or green, bright or dull. Nothing mattered. The play was over! She had passed a test — of all her freshman tests the hardest, of all the tests she had ever taken the hardest.

Immediately Bonnie felt a difference in the atmosphere of Broad Harbor High School. Girls and boys who had scarcely looked at her before called out "Hi, Bonnie" when they saw her. Tom Farr, the most popular boy in school, had a "Hi" for her. Norma, embarrassed over her stage fright, avoided Bonnie as much as possible that week. Gone was that patronizing air. It seemed fairly certain that she would never call her "the little island girl" again.

96

12. Jimmy Is Different

WAS that Jimmy? Bonnie asked herself. That tall young man in the dark suit, with slicked-down hair? That serious young man up there on the platform making a speech? It was certainly his voice. And who but Jimmy Daniels could talk like that about boatbuilding in the early days on the Maine coast, as if nothing ever had been or ever could be quite so important as boats?

Bonnie, Island Girl

Two school years had gone by. It was June and here was Jimmy graduating from Easton High School. Here was Bonnie practically a junior, and sixteen years old.

The boy on the platform finished his speech and sat down. Bonnie clapped till her palms tingled, and he looked out over rows of heads and grinned right at her for an instant — the same old Jimmy. He was the same old Jimmy when she saw him at the end of the program and gave him her present — a fountain pen.

"Gee, Bonnie, thanks! Just what I'll need on the job this summer."

When they went home to Bayberry Island next day on the mail boat he was as usual full of plans. He was going to work all summer in a boatshop down Boston way. It was run by a friend of Fred Murphy's, the man he'd worked for in Easton, and he'd have a chance to learn an awful lot down there. In September he would start going to night school. He was going to study draftsmanship and all about diesel engines and a number of other things.

They sat up in front of the pilothouse in glaring sunlight. Yet a shadow seemed to fall across the girl's face. She looked at him gravely. "We won't be seeing much of you on Bayberry after this."

"Sure you will. I'll keep coming back. Anyway, *you*

can see a lot of me next week if you want to. I don't leave till the week after. Why don't we go places and do things?"

"Say we do, Jimmy."

On Monday night, just as Bonnie was starting upstairs to bed, the *Water Spider* came skittering into Pretty Cove. Jimmy dashed up the slope and into the Andrews's kitchen to announce between panting breaths, "Mackerel's running! Bates Inlet — Pa's going out — Can't Bonnie come along — starting right away."

"Oh *can* I, Pa? *Can* I?"

She had never been on a night fishing trip before. The few times her father had been out with Henry McAdam on his seiner, he had always said they'd be too busy to take kids along and that they might be out all night and Bonnie ought to get her sleep. So it was all new — this voyage into darkness for silver treasure, this race to get to the fishing grounds first. All around them was the sound of throbbing engines. The seiners were rushing out from island villages, for word had just come over the radio that mackerel were running.

When the big seiner entered Bates Inlet, the lights were turned off. They moved slowly and silently through the darkness, like conspirators. Bonnie felt as if she were taking part in a pursuit of secret treasure under cover of night. Now she could see the treasure they were after. It glowed ahead of them — molten silver under the surface of the water.

The men began paying out the great net with its line of cork floats along the top. First it hung straight down like a curtain. Slowly the curtain began to curve as the men drew the purse lines tighter and tighter, folding the net gently around the school of fishes.

Bonnie held her breath. Could they get the bottom closed in time? Or would the fish take fright as they felt the twine drawing in around them and rush out to freedom just before the trap closed? She had seen many a seiner come home empty because the men hadn't been quick enough.

"We've got 'em! Slathers of them!" they shouted.

Bonnie let out her breath. The men bent to the backbreaking task of scooping up the fish in small nets out of the bulging net which floated beside the seiner. There was no more acting like a bunch of burglars. They laughed and joked as they ladled flapping mackerel onto the deck. Yet they wasted not a moment of time. The first boats back to the fish wharf at Easton with a load would get top prices. Even a little delay could mean a price drop if there was a big run. The men sweat in the cool night air.

They sang as they speeded toward the mainland with a cargo of silver. Engines sounded behind them. As yet none throbbed ahead of them. Bonnie grew tense, as if she herself were running a race. Eagerly she watched the miles of water retreat behind them and the long, dark mass of mainland draw slowly nearer. Three miles more. Two miles. One mile. Half a mile. Now nothing but the engine's breaking down could keep theirs from being the first boat in — with hundreds of pounds of fish. The powerful engine beat on. The wharf came out to meet them. The seiner slid alongside. A great shout burst at the same moment from everybody on board.

"We didn't come home till morning," sang Bonnie and Jimmy as they rushed into the lighted kitchen where Pa ate his early breakfast.

Ma set out two more plates. "Have a good time?" she asked.

"Wonderful!" "Terrific!" they chorused.

That whole week was "wonderful" and "terrific."

One day they went to see Susan at Black Cove on Woods Island. It took a little hunting to find that particular cove on an island that is almost all coves and inlets. But find it they did. It looked a little like Pretty Cove and Susan's house looked much like

Bonnie's. A girl came out and stood watching the strange boat come in. She was tall and slender, with light hair, and she wore a blue dress.

"Hi, Susan! Hi, Susan!" shouted Bonnie.

"It's Bonnie!" yelled Susan after the girl in the *Water Spider* had nearly waved an arm off. She came flying down to the landing, followed by a procession of brothers and sisters.

Bonnie had never visited her Woods Island friend before. Yet she at once felt at home. So did Jimmy. "A picnic! A picnic!" the youngsters chorused at the sight of the hot dogs and rolls the visitors had brought. "Come on, let's get a fire started on the beach." They scurried around like a lot of ants. The Bayberry Islanders had brought enough to feed the whole family and then some. Still Susan's mother kept thinking of something to add to the feast. How about some of her mustard pickle? And they must have some pie. Those pies were hot out of the oven. Susan would get some Cokes at the store. No, Ben could get the Cokes while Susan helped butter rolls.

Within a half hour Bonnie, Jimmy, and all the young Millers plus a couple of their friends were gathered around a fire, roasting and eating hot dogs and a number of other foods washed down with pop and Cokes.

"We'll have to start back by four sure," Jimmy announced. "If we don't get by Moulton's Reef before half tide we'll have to go clear out around Black and Long and that takes hours and hours."

It was after four-thirty before they actually shoved off. "I'll have to push the little old *Spider* hard," said Jimmy.

Perhaps he pushed too hard. Just within sight of the long reef the *Water Spider* coughed, sputtered, stopped and refused to start again. For two hours Jimmy tinkered with the motor. For two hours he and Bonnie watched Moulton's Reef, like a mastodon's skeleton, rising higher and higher out of the sea. When at last the regular purr was heard once more, the reef lay all exposed, blocking their way home.

They had to turn around and go back by Woods Island, by the long side of the half-moon that was Black Island, out around Long Island. The light of even a long June day was beginning to fade before this detour was completed.

Jimmy looked at the gulls flying purposefully now all in one direction, toward their roosting places on Gull Island, rubbed the sweat off his forehead with his arm and said, "Gee! Hope your Ma won't worry."

Bonnie saw how the water ahead was turning a dull gray. She wasn't hopeful about Ma's not worrying.

"Are you starved?" he asked, when the stars began to prick through overhead.

"Not after all the hot dogs I ate this noon," she answered cheerfully. Yet she was glad of the crumpled-looking chocolate bar he pulled out of his sweater pocket.

Now the islands were dark and fuzzy-edged and all alike except for size. They melted into each other so that it was almost impossible to tell where one ended and another began. Could Jimmy ever find Bayberry in this watery maze? Would they have to wander about till daylight? He was not saying a word now. He just sat, watching, watching. Did he know where they were or was he as lost as she felt? It was impossible to tell from looking at him.

"Look, Bonnie!" The boy spoke suddenly. Out ahead of them a light blinked on and off, stayed dark for the space of three seconds, then shone out once, twice. It was Bayberry Island Light — still several miles ahead but in sight to steer by. "I thought it was about time we saw that little old blinker," said Jimmy.

She ought to have known, the girl told herself, that Jimmy wouldn't get lost. He knew these waterways as well as the night herons did. The light grew steadily bigger. Then Cranberry Point — good old Cranberry Point — came into view.

Jimmy Is Different

"Did you worry, Ma?" asked Bonnie as she and Jimmy sat at the kitchen table wolfing a midnight meal.

Her mother smiled and shook her head. "Your Pa said you'd probably have to come home the long way but that Jimmy'd make it all right." Snores from the next room bore witness to Pa's freedom from worry.

"The first thing I buy with the money I earn this summer," vowed the boy, "will sure be a new motor for the *Spider*. I'm not going to have her acting up like that again when I take someone out." He spoke as he might of a member of his family who had embarrassed him before company.

All that June week the two kept on the move — fishing, picnicking, exploring. They scarcely stayed ashore at all except to eat and sleep and often they ate on the boat or on some beach or rocky point. It ended Saturday night with an evening at the movies in the town hall. Neither the girl nor the boy said much as they came the long way home — the water route. Both felt a letdown. The feeling grew worse the nearer they came to Bonnie's house.

"Good-by, *Water Spider*," the girl said when she stepped out on the beach. "You've given us a swell time this week."

"Guess you and I'll have to say good-by tonight

too," announced Jimmy gravely. "I'll be off by six tomorrow to get the morning bus for Boston."

There was a moment's silence. "Well," said Bonnie, "I've had a wonderful time."

"So've I."

Another silence.

Then Jimmy spoke again. "I'll be back the week before Labor Day. Why can't we have some fun then?"

"Let's do."

"Don't go off now visiting your Long Island cousins or anybody."

"I'll be right here."

"I'll get me that new motor for the *Spider* by then. Boy! There'll be no stopping us. We can go up and down the coast and out to Seal Rock Light — *any-place*."

"That'll be wonderful."

"Good-by Bonnie."

"Good-by Jimmy."

He turned to go, then changed his mind. Putting his arm around her shoulders, he gave her a quick, shy kiss, then pushed the *Water Spider* off quickly and jumped in. Jimmy the matter-of-fact, Jimmy the reserved, *was* different this summer.

13. Everything Is Different

EVERYTHING was different this summer. Bonnie had passed her sixteenth birthday. That was a milestone. She would be an upperclassman in the fall — another milestone. Jimmy at eighteen looked twenty and acted like a real boy friend instead of an older brother.

Pretty Cove was changed. That finger of earth and rock called Cranberry Point was now a summer place.

A low, modernistic house sprawled out over it. A stone terrace overlooked the Cove, complete with outdoor fireplace, bright-colored chairs and tables, and sun umbrellas like huge, exotic flowers. Where blueberries and cranberries once grew, lawn grass sprouted and a flower garden was in the making. Wherever a dweller in Pretty Cove went he was conscious of the Watson place — on the beach, on the rocks, out in a boat, over at the Harbor. From every angle the old Point wore a new look.

The Watsons would arrive the first of July. So Nellie Foster, the postmistress, said. She showed everybody the stacks of letters and packages for the new residents. The stacks grew higher with every mail. "Have to build an addition on this place if the stuff keeps coming in," she said.

Then the mail boat began bringing huge express packages addressed to the newcomers. Presently the *Summer Wind* put in with a load of furniture. She made two more trips. Promptly on the first of July the family came with trunks, bags, baskets and cartons and an Irish setter to which Chummy took an instant dislike. Now at the Pretty Cove moorings, alongside the sturdy lobster boats, the *Summer Wind* lay at anchor, gleaming in the sunlight by day and showing a light in her rigging like a new planet by night.

Everything Is Different

Bonnie wondered if Greg would remember "Bonnie Jean from Pretty Cove." He had said he wouldn't forget her. Yet that was two years ago. Last summer, when the house was being built, he had not come to Bayberry at all. Two years is a long time and summer folks had a reputation for short memories. It looked as though Greg had even forgotten Andrews Village. The lighthouse and all the little houses and toy-sized boats, which he had asked Bonnie to take care of for him, still lay in a box in her closet, unclaimed. The weir was falling to pieces, the dam was full of holes.

As for Betty and the twins they never went there now. They had a village of their own practically in their front yard and they were — with considerable help from Pa — making new boats to moor in its harbor.

"Cap'n Hill and Cap'n Bailey and Cap'n Swan all live in Pretty Cove now," announced Betty. "They like it better here. It's nearer for the girls to go to school." Education loomed large in Betty's mind. She had just finished her first year at Bayberry Island School.

Why shouldn't I use the little cove, thought Bonnie. She could fix it up a bit and go there just as she used to when she wanted to be away from the kids to read or to think by herself. So one warm afternoon, tucking a book under her arm, she set off through the woods. Coming to the edge of the cove, the girl stood still suddenly and listened. Someone was there! She peeked through the branches of the low-bending spruce. A mottled patch of reds and greens glowed out of the shadows like a garden of tropical blossoms, misplaced among gray New England rocks. She made out a squatting figure. The flower bed was evidently on the back of this person — a sport shirt.

Bonnie retreated. In her hurry she stepped on a stone which went rolling into the water. Quickly a head and a pair of shoulders were thrust through the branches of the tree. It was Greg, grown tall, grown even better-looking than he had been two years ago. A bright smile flashed out at sight of her. "Why, it's Bonnie Jean! You're the person I've been wanting to see. Where you been keeping yourself?"

"Home," she said briefly.

"Come and help me fix up our village." He sounded as if they were joint owners. "I want this place to look just the way it used to. I can do the dam, but I'm dog-goned if I can get the hang of that fish weir."

"I've still got all those boats and little houses in my closet. I was wondering if you'd forgotten them."

"Not me. Didn't forget *you* either."

She began gathering small sticks for the weir. As

110

the two worked they talked. Or rather, Greg talked. Bonnie made brief, shy answers to his questions. How had she liked going to Broad Harbor to school? Why didn't her brothers and sister play here? Would she come back tomorrow and help him some more? And the next day? And the next? Wouldn't she show him all her favorite places this summer? Was Porcupine Hill one? Would she climb it with him? Where was that cave he'd heard about? Would she take him there? How about coming with them on a cruise? They often went out for several days at a time on the *Summer Wind*. He'd ask his mother to invite her. *Would* she come?

When he stopped for breath the girl felt out of breath too. She did not commit herself to anything except that she would be back tomorrow to help him. She was going to be terribly busy picking berries. Wild raspberries were getting ripe. Then blueberries would be coming along and after that blackberries. "I have to earn all I can in summer," she told him.

"I like to pick berries. I'll help you."

"Ma and the kids will help me."

Her unresponsiveness did not discourage the boy in the least. "See you tomorrow, Bonnie Jean," he called after her cheerfully when she said good-by abruptly and set out for home.

When she got to the house, Bonnie felt as if she had been heading into a stiff breeze for the past two hours.

A few days later Pa sounded a warning. "Now don't you go getting thick with that Watson boy, Bonnie." He had just seen Greg walking back with her from Secret Cove. "That boy came on the *Summer Wind* and he'll go away on the fall wind and when winter winds blow he'll forget all about you and everybody else on Bayberry Island. That's the way with summer folks."

"I don't *intend* to get thick with him," said Bonnie firmly, and meant it. No summer boy was going to turn *her* head. She would just help him put the little village together again for her own satisfaction.

The job in Secret Cove took longer than Bonnie had anticipated. Greg talked more than he worked. Did he dawdle on purpose? She began to suspect so. After several days she found herself wanting to prolong this joint enterprise. The boy's gaiety and enthusiasm were catching. It was fun to do things with him. She came back from the little cove singing. She felt like dancing through the woods.

Somehow Greg made her feel like that. He sparkled. He wore bells. He was not like anyone she had ever known before. Set him down among all those

112

boys and girls at Broad Harbor and within a day or two he'd be the most popular boy in the school, more popular even than Tom Farr, captain of the football team, who was every Broad Harbor girl's dream date All the same, he needn't think she was going to give him a lot of her time this summer. She had other things to do besides fool around with a handsome summer boy.

In spite of this resolve, Bonnie saw more and more of Greg Watson. It was hard to say "No" to him, for he always expected "Yes." He was a lot like the Andrews dog. If you shook a stick at Chummy and said "Go home," he never believed you meant it. He just frisked and barked hilariously and expected you to throw the stick for him to fetch. In the same way Greg never took seriously "No," or "I'm sorry but I can't go," or "I'm going to be busy tomorrow."

One afternoon when the two were at work, Mrs. Watson appeared in a rowboat, bringing ice cream and cookies. Like Greg, she sparkled with enthusiasm and high spirits. She seemed amazingly young and pretty to be anybody's mother. So this was the little cove she'd heard so much about. What a perfect place! And the toy village was charming. Just as soon as they got settled she intended to come here often. She would bring her sewing over. They must have picnics here. She would ask Elmer, the man who worked on their place, to make some rustic seats and put them under that wonderful old spruce tree, and a table too. And she simply loved that name — Secret Cove.

It certainly wouldn't be a secret cove much longer, thought Bonnie.

The Watsons gave a housewarming. Everybody on Bayberry Island was invited. The summer people all accepted. So did many of the young people among the islanders. Few of the parents attended. Why spend an evening with perfect strangers? they asked. The only ones who went from Pretty Cove were Mrs. Andrews, who wanted to "see what kind of folks those Watsons were," and Mrs. Collins — with Mabel, of course — because the Watsons had done "considerable trading" at her store and she hoped they'd keep it up.

Bonnie had so much fun she hated to have the evening over. Her mother was a bored, uncomfortable, anxious wallflower. In spite of the efforts of the Watsons to give everybody a good time, she stayed on the side lines, speaking only when spoken to and then in monosyllables. Impatiently she waited for Bonnie to be ready to go home.

"Those folks'll get you discontented and envious,

114

making such a fuss over you," was the first thing she said on the way back to the Cove.

"But they envy me, Ma. Honest they do. Greg and his mother and his pa all say they wish they lived on Bayberry all the time."

"What's stopping them if they really want to? Just their own softness." Her mother's voice was scornful.

Summers were never long enough. This one ran a race. The days seemed shorter than December days. Bonnie and the twins, with considerable help from Ma and spasmodic help from Betty, picked hundreds of quarts of raspberries, blueberries and blackberries and sold them to Whalers' Inn and to summer cottagers. Bonnie made enough money as her share to buy herself the new pumps she needed and some material as flowery as one of Greg's shirts to make herself a billowy skirt. Then there were the usual canning and pickle-making. A fruity, spicy smell hung over the kitchen every year from July to September, and this summer was no exception. Between picking berries, peddling them and canning them, Bonnie had little time left over. What there was Greg stood ready to fill to the brim. He was always coming up with a suggestion. How about her showing him how to get to such and such a place? She and the twins were going fishing? Couldn't he go too? How about a game of badminton? She didn't know how to play? He'd teach her. It was easy. His mother wanted to know if she would have supper with them tonight on the *Summer Wind*.

If Ma had been a dog she would have growled deep down in her throat at the Watsons, just the way Chummy did at the Watson's red setter. She wished they had never come here on their handsome boat. She wished they would let Bonnie alone. They would spoil her.

As for the girl, she felt breathless most of the time. In August came the climax of this exciting summer — an invitation to take a four- or five-day cruise along the coast. A cruise on the *Summer Wind!* Could anything so wonderful actually happen to her?

"No. It couldn't," said Ma firmly.

Pa felt the same way. She was not going off with folks that were "practically strangers." How did she know that they could handle a boat? What did they know about this coast? Might end up on Moulton's Reef or Skeleton Point.

"But they've got Cap'n Reed. He was born somewhere around here and he's been sailing Mr. Watson's boats for years."

"If you want a boat trip I'll take you on one. I'll run you all over Sunday to Long Island to see the cousins. We'll do our cruising in the little old *Anne Marie.*"

A trip with the family to Long Island on Pa's lobster boat! How *could* he think that would make up for refusing this wonderful invitation? A door to glorious adventure had opened for her — only to slap to in her face.

"Oh-h-h! I've never in my life had a chance to take a trip on a boat like that and I never will again — *never,* and you won't let me go!" protested Bonnie wildly, tearfully.

Pa picked up the lobster trap he had been mending on the doorstep and walked off down to the cove as if he had not heard a word she said. She would get nowhere with him by talking as if the *Anne Marie* wasn't good enough for her.

She dropped the subject. But she brought it up again the next day and the next and the day after that. Whenever and wherever she had both parents together she talked about that cruise. She also pleaded with them separately. Finally, sick of the subject, sick of the very name *Summer Wind,* Pa weakened.

"All right if you want to cruise around with summer folks, go ahead. At least they've got a cap'n that knows his business." He had been making inquiries about Captain Reed.

"You haven't anything fit to wear on a trip like that," Ma objected, hoping this would dampen the girl's enthusiasm. It didn't.

She wouldn't need much. Mrs. Watson said there'd be no dressing up. They would live in slacks and dungarees. She wouldn't need anything new except the flowery skirt to put on with a white blouse in the evening and she could finish that skirt in another day.

So Bonnie washed the berry stains out of her dungarees, washed some blouses and her red sweater, hemmed the new skirt that had pictures scattered over it — red and green pictures — and was all set for the trip on the *Summer Wind.*

Twice the cruise had to be postponed. Once Mr. Watson had to go away on business. Again, a three-day storm kept the schooner in the cove. August was rushing by. Perhaps they wouldn't go at all, worried Bonnie. Then there came a clear blue Saturday morning. At seven o'clock Greg dashed across the Point to shout, "Oh, Bonnie, can you be ready by nine o'clock?"

"Sure can," said Bonnie.

The graceful schooner unfurled her sails and ran with the wind out of Pretty Cove, out around Cranberry Point. The minute the island girl had stepped over the rail, she began living a beautiful dream.

118

Everything Is Different

Everything about this floating toy house was unreal. The little stateroom, shared with Evelyn Wells, another guest, had pink and blue chintz curtains at the windows and its own tiny bathroom. The galley, about the size of a clothes closet, with shelves that pulled out of the walls and tables that let down and folded up again. The delicious meals prepared in that galley and eaten from another table that let down in the saloon or from a table set up under an awning on deck. The tinkling ship's bell, which made the passing of time seem unreal. The soft-cushioned deck chairs, which invited loafing. The new games she learned to play. Nothing was like real life — not as Bonnie knew it, anyway.

She had expected to feel ill at ease, especially with her fellow guests — these old friends and neighbors of the Watsons from Connecticut. Would this girl Evelyn turn out to be another Norma? She didn't. Everybody on board took the attitude: We're all here together for a few days like one family. Let's be informal and friendly and have fun. Bonnie did not know how to play the deck games they played or to dance the dances they danced, but nobody treated her like an ignoramus and Greg was a more than willing teacher. She learned fast under his encouraging tutoring.

Bonnie, Island Girl

Sunday night, one hundred miles from Pretty Cove, she suddenly remembered something. *This was the last week in August* — the week Jimmy was coming home! She had promised to go all up and down the coast with him on the *Water Spider* — a *Spider* with a new motor. In her excitement over this trip she had forgotten — it seemed incredible — all about Jimmy and his plans. What *would* he think of her?

She would write him a letter this minute and explain. She must be sure to mail it at Riverport when they put in there tomorrow morning. *What* to say? Certainly not that she had forgotten. He must never know that. Sitting down at the desk in the saloon, she wrote:

DEAR JIMMY:

I'm taking the most wonderful trip. The Watsons invited me to go with them on the *Summer Wind* and I accepted, for I knew I'd never get another chance all my life to sail on a boat like her.

Expected to leave three weeks ago but they put off going twice. Sorry I won't be home to say hello when you come back, but we'll be sailing into Pretty Cove Wednesday night and that will give you and me time to have some fun on the *Water Spider* before we both have to go away again.

Be seeing you!

BONNIE

120

Everything Is Different

Almost as soon as she dropped the letter into the mailbox at Riverport the next morning, the girl wished she could pull it out again. What had possessed her to suggest that a trip with summer folks on a fancy schooner could be more fun than going places with Jimmy on his pride and joy, the *Water Spider?* He'd be terribly hurt. Well, she'd fix things up with him somehow when they were together again. Still, she wished she'd thought more before writing that note.

Bonnie was not thinking these days. She was dreaming.

14. Living in a Dream

THE Bayberry Island girl dreamed on, as one shining day followed another. The *Summer Wind* idled along, exploring this cove, poking into that inlet, settling down each night at a new mooring. The voyagers went ashore whenever they felt like it to sun themselves on a sandy beach, to fish, to go to the movies. Bonnie liked best the fishing expeditions because those gave *her* a chance to shine. She seldom beat anybody at shuffleboard. Her dance steps were limited. She couldn't swim as well as the others did, even if she did live on an island, and she couldn't dive at all. But she knew where to find the fish and when the young folks dangled their lines over the side of the schooner or off a rocky point she was always the one who pulled in the most.

Home, Pa, Ma and the kids seemed two thousand miles away. Pretty Cove was a place she used to live in long ago, before this lovely life began. The moonlight on the water never looked so beautiful at home. Was that just a lantern hanging on the mast at night? It looked like a star that had fallen out of the sky and caught in the rigging. How she hated to see the boat turn on Tuesday and head up-coast again!

The shining days ended suddenly — in a smothering fog. On Wednesday morning Bonnie looked out of the stateroom window into a grayish-white curtain that shut down a few feet beyond the gunwale. Wisps of mist clung to the top of the tall mast. Muffled whistles and horns were the only signs of life in this unsubstantial world.

"We'll have to sit right here till the fog lifts," announced the captain.

The schooner sat the morning out. At noon, with furled sails, she crawled along for a few hours, blowing her horn as she crawled. By four o'clock the captain dropped anchor again. This was the day they had expected to be home. She had written Jimmy so.

She had told Ma so. Oh, well, they all knew there was nothing to do in a fog like this but wait. The *Summer Wind* would be back in Pretty Cove tomorrow night for sure.

It was still foggy on Thursday morning. However, the curtains were thinner and hung higher. "We'll round Cranberry Point tonight if it gets no worse," the skipper prophesied hopefully. The fog proceeded to retreat toward the horizon, and by midmorning the *Summer Wind* was on her way. By noon white banks far out to sea were all that remained of the thick weather. Yet Captain Reed did not look relieved. He looked anxious. Something seemed to be seriously wrong with the engine. The schooner labored along.

Mr. Watson and the skipper held long consultations above the cockpit, like doctors gravely studying a patient. They decided to call in a specialist.

"Best man I know is fifteen miles back at Bennett's Harbor," said Captain Reed. They turned the boat around and started back.

The *Summer Wind* crawled to Bennett's Harbor and they spent the night there. Next morning — it was Friday now — the captain rowed the dory ashore in search of a trouble shooter. In about an hour he came back with a repairman, who presently announced that he'd have to go ashore again to get something he needed for the job.

Not till well into that afternoon was the *Summer Wind* her old purring self. "Anyway, we'll be home for Sunday," Greg said cheerfully, "and Dad telephoned to Ellery Johnson's boat over at Bayberry about our being held up and said to make sure your folks got word. So what do you look so sober for? You've not a thing to worry about. Come on, let's have a game of shuffleboard."

"Nothing to worry about! That's what *you* think," said the Bayberry Island girl, but she did not say it aloud. Greg didn't care, none of the others cared when they got back to Pretty Cove. But wouldn't she have a time explaining everything to Jimmy!

He probably had the *Water Spider* all scrubbed up and ready. He was eager to show off her paces with the new motor. Bonnie could see him with his forehead wrinkled up and hear him say in a puzzled tone, "But Bonnie, I thought you told me you'd be right here all this week." Then he'd fix those frank blue eyes on her and she'd own up that she had forgotten and he would be surprised and sore. He was one of those people who always do what they say they'll do. He couldn't possibly understand how a girl could lose her head over a trip on a boat like the *Summer Wind* and forget everything and everybody else for a little while. She just must think of something to say that would square herself with him.

"Hey! what's the matter with your aim today?" sang out Greg. "You're shooting all over the deck."

Bonnie forced herself to pay attention to the game.

Late on Saturday afternoon the *Summer Wind* at last rounded Cranberry Point. The twins and Betty came down to the beach on a run. Ma followed them. Mabel Collins was already there. Bonnie went over the side of the schooner into the dory. The dream ended.

"Had quite a trip, didn't you?" said Mrs. Andrews. Her kiss was warm but her voice held stored-up disapproval. So did the glance she cast in the direction of the *Summer Wind.* "Next time you want to go on a cruise you'd better let your Pa take you on the *Anne Marie.* She's not so pretty nor so speedy but at least she gets you home on time. And so does the *Water Spider* with her brand-new motor."

"Seen anything of Jimmy?" asked Bonnie quickly.

"Sure I've seen him. He didn't know what to make of you — going off like that after saying you'd be here this week — and I didn't either. Says he guesses he can't compete with summer folks and their boats."

"I'm sorry about Jimmy. I just plain forgot. Guess I'd better go over to his house and explain."

"You won't do any explaining to Jimmy. He left on the mail boat this morning."

"When's he coming back?"

"Next Christmas. Maybe by that time you'll have your head on your shoulders again."

"You mean he's gone *to Boston?*"

That was exactly what Ma meant.

"But I thought he was going to be here till Labor Day. Why did he leave so soon?"

A laugh as mocking as a sea gull's cry followed Bonnie and her mother up the path to the cottage. It was Mabel Collins's. She sat on a rock below and laughed and laughed.

So many things seemed funny to that girl!

15. End of a Summer

"SEE you at Christmas time *sure*. Don't forget to answer my letters."

It was Greg Watson speaking. He had come running over from Cranberry Point just as Captain Taylor shouted, "All aboa-r-rd!" Now he stood on the wharf beside Ma and the kids and smiled down at Bonnie while the mail boat got under way.

The girl smiled back. She was off for Broad Harbor, saying good-by to the family once more, ready to start her junior year in high school. This time there was no Jimmy going along. But there was Greg to see her off.

End of a Summer

"It's been a wonderful summer," he shouted.

Everything about the slim, tanned boy looked golden-brown as he stood there in the morning sunlight waving good-by. His crew-cut hair, his hazel eyes, his sun-bronzed skin — all were the same color. He had never looked so handsome before to the eyes of the small, dark girl looking at him across a widening strip of water.

"It's been a wonderful summer!" called passengers around her to friends on shore. They were summer visitors reluctantly going back to the city.

Yes, it had been a wonderful summer, thought Bonnie. She sat down on her suitcase and let out a long sigh of relief. It seemed like the first long breath she had taken since the beginning of July. Perhaps now that the wonderful summer was over she could stop feeling breathless, confused and pulled in two directions at once, toward home and away from home, toward Greg and toward Jimmy. The Watson boy had given her in eight weeks more fun than she had known in all the rest of her summers if you piled all their weeks on top of each other. Yet always with this new friend she felt separated from her old friends, from her old life. At the house on Cranberry Point, on board the *Summer Wind*, even in Pretty Cove — when Greg was there — she seemed to be taking part

129

in a play or living a dream. Then he would go home or she would go back to the Andrews cottage and be in the real world again, where a girl did housework and picked berries and looked after Betty.

Ma and Pa had added to her breathlessness. They kept telling her she was a "little fool to let that handsome summer boy give her such a whirl. He could talk a fish out of the water, that boy could." They said he would sail off in September and forget all about her and next summer he would find another girl to rush.

Well, they were all wrong about Greg. He was going to write to her and had asked her to write to him. He planned to come back for Christmas and wanted to see her then for sure. He liked her better than any of the girls he knew at home. He told her so that last day on the *Summer Wind*.

"Bonnie, when we get there will you show me where Birch Street is? That's where I'm going to live." A rather small voice spoke at her elbow.

It was Anne Lundberg. She was entering Broad Harbor High this year. One look at the girl's anxious face brought back to Bonnie all her own fears of two years ago. She knew exactly how Anne was feeling.

"We'll go over there together. Birch is near Pine

Street and I live on Pine. In fact everything's pretty near together in Broad Harbor. You'll see."

"Oh-h-h thanks. It would be terrible to get lost in a big town like that."

"You can't get lost in Broad Harbor, not really lost. Anyway, I'll pick you up tomorrow morning and look after you."

The other girl's relief was plain to see. Yet she still had much on her mind. "Will those mainland boys and girls act like I didn't know anything? Will they poke fun at me?"

"No. Not if you keep your chin up and act like you know your way around."

Keep your chin up. That was what Jimmy had told her two years ago. She had been just as scared then as Anne was now, a "little island girl" venturing into a new world — a big high school in a big mainland town. Hadn't Jimmy been wonderful that day! He had stayed on the boat to Broad Harbor and seen her to 24 Pine Street. She had felt all through those first weeks that he was betting on her. He had come over to be a cheering section of one and seen her through that frightful ordeal of acting in the school play — acting opposite Norma. He never told her she was pretty or cute, or that he was crazy about her, the way Greg did. Jimmy didn't talk much anyway. Yet

131

always he seemed standing by like a Coast Guard boat.

Nothing ought to come between two such old friends. She had written him a long letter yesterday. She watched the mail for his handwriting.

Jimmy answered promptly, also briefly — two lines on a post card. His letters, like his talks, had always been brief. This one was telegraphic:

> Don't give last summer another thought and I won't either. Got plenty to think about right here.
>
> JIMMY

Why, *why* couldn't he understand how a girl could get excited in August and forget something she said in June? He just didn't try to see her side of it.

Well, that was that! He had plenty to think about, did he? So had she. Junior year was going to be busy all right, with chorus practice and basketball — not to mention baby-sitting and homework. She could get along perfectly without Jimmy. He'd *see*.

A letter from Greg arrived that first week too. It was a long letter. He missed her. What fun they'd had last summer, more fun than he ever had at home. He wished he lived on an island all the time. He wished he had her next door all the year round. Anyway, he really was going to spend Christmas vacation on Bay-

berry. Dad and mother had promised that they would
open up the Cranberry Point house and have a country Christmas. He hoped there'd be lots of snow and
good skiing. Could she ski? He'd teach her if she
couldn't. Wouldn't she write soon and tell him how
she liked being a junior? And so on for several pages.

He enclosed some snapshots taken aboard the
Summer Wind to "keep you from forgetting that
trip." As if she ever could forget it!

She went through the snapshots slowly. There they
all were on the deck of the *Summer Wind* — Mr. and
Mrs. Watson, Greg, the Wellses, the captain, the cook
and a girl with dancing eyes. That was she! Here were
Greg and Evelyn Wells and her brother playing
shuffleboard. There was Greg diving off the deck into
Black Rock Cove. Here was Bonnie again, holding up
a big flounder. She looked the pictures through once,
then went right through again. She stood them up
in a row along the back of her desk. They looked like
the cast of a musical comedy played on the deck of
the Good Ship *Summer Wind*.

16. The Big Storm

THE big storm came the day after Thanksgiving,
came on a southeast wind. Ma, Bonnie and the
twins were "boughing" the house that morning. They
were laying spruce boughs, which Mr. Andrews had
cut, all around the foundations and weighing them
down with boards and stones to keep the house warm
through a long winter. They hurried to finish the job
before those black clouds out beyond Seal Island got
any nearer.

"Wish your Pa had had sense enough not to go out
this morning. I see Henry McAdam didn't go," Ma
fretted.

"He'll be all right," Bonnie reassured her. "He's seen this coming. He always watches the sky."

As she spoke a gust of wind tore the bough she held out of her hands and carried it across the yard. Whew! that wind was getting strong. How suddenly it had come! Then she saw how the boats in Pretty Cove were cavorting up and down and how white water broke high in the air over Cranberry Point. Ma saw these things too and her eyes darkened with anxiety.

"He'll be all right," said Bonnie again.

Ma always worried like this when Pa was out in a storm. Yet he always came through. He had come through that terrific storm which people still talked about, when the old mail boat was driven onto Moulton's Reef and battered to pieces, when wreckage was strewn for miles up and down the coast. He had taken refuge that time on the leeward side of Woods Island. Bonnie had been a little girl then, but she could still remember her mother walking back and forth, back and forth, from the kitchen window to the chair by the stove, still see her peering through the panes toward Cranberry Point. She had actually worn the paint off the floor boards that day.

By early afternoon Ma was pacing the kitchen floor again, back and forth from stove or sink or table to the window. By then the boats anchored in the Cove were acting like a herd of frightened horses and geysers of water broke over the Point.

Presently it was impossible to see the Cove. The rain *swooshed* against the windows as if a giant hurled it in great handfuls at the house. Still Mrs. Andrews peered out. Even when she was not by the window her eyes seemed to be fixed on the distance.

"He said when he started extra early he'd get back before the storm was bad, even if he had to skip some of the traps," she thought out loud, "but the storm got bad so fast, faster'n he or anybody else expected."

"He's seen it coming and put in somewhere, just the way he did that other time."

Bonnie spoke to someone who did not hear.

By suppertime nobody in the little box of a house was talking except Betty. She asked over and over, "When's Pa going to get home?"

"Just as soon as he can, Betty." Ma kept her voice cheerful, but anxiety was in every line of her face. It clouded her eyes.

They kept the radio turned on. The reports coming over the air were anything but reassuring. Boats missing. Boats aground. The *Ellen D.* — and the *Sea Wolf* — swept from their moorings in Fog Harbor. A big carrier from the Easton herring cannery was sending out an SOS. And those big cannery boats always seemed equal to anything! Bonnie felt, as she sat and listened to the storm outside and the voices of the fishermen and Coast Guard men, that she herself was out there on the dark wind-swept water.

"If the *Anne Marie* only had a radio!" sighed Ma under her breath.

"So that Pa could send an SOS," Bonnie finished to herself.

Nobody wanted to go to bed and nobody was sent to bed. Betty played on the floor with her doll until, suddenly, sleep caught up with her and she toppled over in a small, limp heap and was carried upstairs, still holding onto Gloria Jean by one leg. The twins said they were going to sit up till Pa came home even if he didn't get there till morning. They changed their minds soon after ten and went upstairs, already half asleep.

Bonnie and her mother sat and waited. They neither talked nor worked. Their hands lay idle but not relaxed in their laps. It seemed strange to see Ma's busy hands unoccupied. Always they were moving — with needle and thread or knitting needles, when the housework was done. The two pairs of eyes — eyes that were so much alike — looked into space. Now and then Ma would get up, go to the woodbox and put a few more sticks in the stove. Then she would sit silent again.

Once Bonnie heard her mother murmur softly, "He maketh the storm a calm, so that the waves thereof are still," and again, "Who hath measured the waters in the hollow of his hand?" For a few minutes Ma sat back easily in her chair, then she jumped up and looked out the window again.

"Bonnie, don't you ever marry a fisherman," she burst forth so suddenly and so fiercely that the girl jumped.

"I never shall, Ma." She spoke almost as fiercely as her mother had.

At eleven Mrs. Andrews took down the coffee percolator from the shelf above the stove and made some coffee. They drank it in silence, in silence, that is, except for the radio voices.

At twelve o'clock Mrs. Joyce ran into the kitchen to tell them that the wind was slackening, that Henry McAdam said they didn't need to worry. Peter Andrews had certainly put in somewhere and was safe.

"But this time it got bad so fast," said Ma, for probably the tenth time since morning.

Again the two sat alone in the kitchen. Gradually they became aware that the house no longer had "the shakes." There had been no howling for at least twenty minutes. "Look!" cried Bonnie from the window. The moon was struggling up over a bank of clouds. The storm had ended. Presently the sky above Pretty Cove was a clear blue-black space and the moon poured down quiet light as if nothing had happened. Only the whitecaps below told of the turbulent hours just past.

"He maketh the storm a calm," repeated Ma.

In spite of the coffee, Bonnie fell asleep, sitting straight in a hard-backed kitchen chair. She awoke to hear her mother calling out to her, "Bonnie! Listen! That's the *Anne Marie's* motor."

Mr. Andrews's face, usually ruddy, was gray-white when he came into the house, staggering from exhaustion. Mrs. Andrews helped him out of dripping oilskins and rubber boots and drew a chair close to the stove for him, then crammed the firebox full of wood. Bonnie did not have to be told to make coffee and set haddock frying. She wanted to sing. Pa had come through the storm. He was safe!

Her mother already looked like a different person. Her face as well as Bonnie's wore a singing look.

In their relief over having Pa home safe neither mother nor daughter gave a thought to what this day must have brought in losses. Pa reminded them. "There's stove-in traps and loose trap buoys strewed from here to the channel. They're piled up six deep alongshore," he announced gloomily between big swallows of coffee. "Bet two thirds of mine are busted. Be lucky if I find thirty whole ones left. Soon's it's daylight I'll have to go out again and see."

Having finished his supper-breakfast, he got up, set the alarm clock for five-thirty, then dropped onto the couch-bed, a dead weight, and was immediately asleep.

They left him there to himself. Ma went upstairs with Bonnie and both crawled into bed with the sleeping Betty. Neither knew anything more till they heard the youngest member of the family calling, "Ma, I'm terrible hungry."

Bonnie and her mother could hardly believe their eyes when they saw how the sun streamed into the room, across the floor and onto the bed.

The twins and Betty had been dressed and outdoors for a couple of hours. They had been beachcombing in the Cove, which the storm had strewn with wonderful things. Their treasures lay heaped up in the woodshed — bottles, shells, torn nets, cork floats, a storm-weary bird with a broken wing, which died almost as soon as they brought him in and was buried with much ceremony, a huge tuna head with gaping eye sockets, which Ma told them to carry right back to the cove as "fast as they could leg it." There was also a collection of wooden buoys which the storm had torn from traps. "Here's one, two, three of Pa's," they exclaimed, pointing excitedly to those with the Andrews mark — one yellow and one black stripe, "and you just ought to see all the busted traps there are down there. Some of them're thrown way up on the Point."

Bonnie looked out the window at a sky almost as blue as a summer sky and at blue water sloshing against the shore. "Doesn't that sea look innocent?" she said disgustedly. "After all the damage it's gone and done."

"Just as innocent as a blue-eyed kitten," her mother agreed with feeling. Then she burst out again as she had the night before. "Don't you ever marry a lobsterman. You can't count on a thing a week ahead. Here I thought this fall, with lobsters plenty and the price still holding up good, we could have a few extras. I even told George Ellis over at the store to save a couple of those boys' plaid wool jackets they've got in for Christmas and one of those cute baby dolls. Now I'll have to tell George to put the jackets and doll back in stock. Thought we'd have quite a Christmas this year. Be lucky now if we have a Christmas dinner."

"Don't tell George to put those things back with the rest — not yet anyhow. Maybe I can earn some extra money over at Broad Harbor somehow. And I never *will* marry a lobsterman," Bonnie promised solemnly.

Sunday afternoon, when Bonnie went back to school on the *Anne Marie*, she still felt like shaking her fist at the ocean stretching satin-smooth ahead of them. Her father had not exaggerated when he estimated that two thirds of his traps were broken or lost. It would take several weeks to replace them all. In the meanwhile the family income was cut just that much.

"I've got to make some extra money between now and Christmas, simply got to," the girl told herself.

17. A Radio Debut

"SUSAN, you can't ever guess what has happened to me. The most wonderful thing!"

"If I can't ever guess, then tell me."

The two girls were walking home from school together.

"It's sort of frightening too, when I stop to think about it."

"Bonnie, will you stop being mysterious and tell me quick what you're going to do?"

"I'm going to sing *on the radio* — on WTNZ — in a contest!"

Susan stopped short. The books tucked under her arm fell to the sidewalk. She looked at her best girl friend as though she had been changed before her eyes into a personage. "Sing on the radio? You're not kidding, are you?"

"Of course I'm not kidding. The chorus is going to sing. We're one of six high school choruses picked from all the high schools in the state of Maine."

"*Oh!* You sounded for a minute like you were the whole show — Bonnie Jean, WTNZ's new vocalist."

"All right. Laugh. But you'd be excited too."

In the quiet of the room on Pine Street, where the two girls joined forces to do their homework, the Bayberry Island girl supplied a few more details. They had been picked out by a sort of talent scout for the radio station. He had come to their Thanksgiving concert from Bellport. Didn't Susan remember that dark man in awfully good-looking clothes whom nobody knew? Some had said he was a newspaper reporter and some said he was some state official. Wouldn't they all have been excited if they'd known what he was there for?

"And just listen to this — the best part's coming! If we're voted the best singers in the contest, we get twenty-five dollars apiece — *apiece,* Susan. Think what having twenty-five dollars just before Christmas means to me this year. I'll get the wool jackets the twins want and Betty's doll and a handbag for Ma. Her old bag's terribly worn. And I'll . . . "

"Don't you spend that money yet," Susan broke in. "You might not get it, you know."

"But I haven't told you about the second prize. That's ten dollars apiece, and I bet we'll get one or the other. We're *good*."

The other girl's shoulders went up in a small shrug, which Bonnie pretended not to see. "What do you say we calm down and do our Spanish?"

"You go ahead, Susan. I've got to write some letters before I do a thing."

She wrote a long letter to Ma and could just see a proud, happy smile widening on her mother's face as she read the news. She longed to write to Jimmy but didn't. She had always shared things like this with him before. But Jimmy wouldn't be interested. Well, she'd write to Greg Watson. *He*'d be interested. He wrote every week. Maybe he would listen in on Saturday the fifteenth to the contest. She did not realize what a comparatively small territory Station WTNZ covered.

Little of Bonnie's homework got done that December day. As a matter of fact her mind was not on studies much of the time during the next two weeks.

145

Sometimes right in the middle of class, or when someone was talking to her, she would be singing in imagination. The chorus practiced long and often. Though it was more than three weeks to Christmas, the high-school building rang with:

> 'Tis the season to be jolly
> Tra-la-la-la-la-la-la-la-la!

and —

> Noel, Noel, Noel, Noel,
> Born is the King of Is-ra-el.

They were trying out carols. The choice took time. It must be a carol they sang well — one not too difficult. Yet they didn't intend to come up with one people heard in the stores and on the streets for weeks before Christmas. Finally, "The Running of the Deer" was selected for this, the first radio appearance of the Broad Harbor High School Chorus.

A few days later Bonnie had still more exciting news to tell Susan, and to write home. "Mr. Parker has picked out four of us to sing the verses and the rest will just come in on the choruses." Mr. Parker was the music teacher and the leader of the chorus. "And I'm the first soprano."

Now at almost any time outside of school hours Bonnie was likely to be practicing —

A Radio Debut

The holly and the ivy,
When they are both full grown,
Of all the trees that are in the wood,
The holly bears the crown —

or one of the other verses of the old carol. The Barnes family soon knew the whole song by heart just from hearing Bonnie sing in her room.

Promptly at seven o'clock on a chilly Saturday morning a bus marked "Chartered" drew up in front of the Broad Harbor High School. The singers in the chorus were there to a man fifteen minutes ahead of time, swinging their arms and slapping themselves to keep warm. Nobody was running any risk of missing the first radio appearance of his life. Bonnie shivered in her woolly brown coat. Whether the shiveriness was due to the cold or the jitters she was not sure, but she certainly hoped nobody guessed how nervous the first soprano felt right now.

The four-hour ride was hilarious. Even the usually quiet boys and girls were keyed up to a high pitch. Bellport was a city, a metropolis compared to Broad Harbor. A few, including Bonnie, had never been in a city before. None had been in Bellport many times. None had ever been in Station WTNZ. For all of them it was the first time behind a mike. Altogether December fifteenth was a big day.

The bus rolled into the outskirts of Bellport. Those most familiar with the city began showing off their familiarity to the others. That tower was a World War II memorial. The big, handsome house up on the hill was the Gus Everhart place. He was the millionaire who was murdered last year. He was buried in the cemetery they just passed. The store over there was Allen & Hall's. You could buy anything, absolutely anything, there. A lobster trap? Well, you could buy the twine for the trap head there.

Suddenly everyone was quiet. The bus had driven up in front of a low building, all glass blocks and shiny chromium. Across the front were the letters WTNZ. In silence they trooped through the heavy plate-glass doors and found themselves in a lobby where buzzers buzzed and people hurried about, timed not to minutes but to seconds. Someone directed the new arrivals to room 220. "Wait there till Mr. Moore sends for you," they were told.

There was much going to lavatories, powder rooms and drinking fountains. There was much fussing with hair and faces. The girls couldn't seem to stop looking at themselves in compact mirrors and asking each other, "Do I look all right?" The boys watched the girls and told them they looked awful, that one had rouge on her nose, another powder on her lips and still another lipstick on her white blouse. Bonnie wished she might have dressed up, but every girl had to wear a white blouse and a navy-blue or black skirt. She had had to borrow a skirt from Susan and it looked, she was sure, much too long for her.

Now a good-looking young man popped in, said, "Hello, boys and girls, you're on in five minutes," then popped out again.

Nervous giggles and more fussing with faces and hair followed the announcement. Bonnie's throat felt very dry. She swallowed and swallowed. It still felt dry. Her face was hot. Her hands were ice-cold. Yet the handkerchief crumpled between her tight palms was soaked with perspiration.

In what seemed more like fifteen minutes than five they were filing into the auditorium and taking their seats on the platform. What an enormous place! It must hold four or five times as many people as the assembly room at school. And it was filled with strangers. At least all those faces seemed strange to Bonnie, as she looked out from the center of the front row of the chorus. There must be a few people she knew out there. Every boy and girl from Broad Harbor High who could get a ride in someone's car or lay hands on bus fare had planned to come and cheer for the "home team." Several mothers and fathers of the singers had driven over. They were lost in the crowd. No one smiled encouragingly as much as to say, "We know what you can do, Bonnie. Go ahead and do it." To the shy girl the people seemed to look at her critically, doubtfully. She pictured all the hundreds, maybe thousands, of invisible strangers who would be listening critically too. Ma and the kids and all the Bayberry Island friends would also be listening, she reminded herself. Yet somehow it was hard from here to picture them.

"And now," said the announcer into a microphone, "we're going to hear from the boys and girls of the Broad Harbor High School." He clapped his hands and the audience politely followed his example.

Mr. Parker stood up, gave the signal for the chorus to rise, then announced, "The Broad Harbor Chorus will sing 'The Running of the Deer.'" He was raising his stick. He was pointing at the four in the center — straight at the first soprano, it seemed to Bonnie.

> The holly and the ivy,
> When they are both full grown . . .

Her voice quavered a little at the beginning. She did hope nobody noticed that quaver. The other three didn't sound quite natural either — not the way they had at rehearsal yesterday. She thought Mr.

Parker looked worried. Were they letting Broad Harbor High down? At last the rest joined in for the chorus.

> The rising of the sun
> And the running of the deer,
> The playing of the merry organ,
> Sweet singing in the choir.

The second verse was much easier and the quartet began to relax and be themselves. They sang the last verse best of all.

> The holly bears a bark
> As bitter as any gall,
> And Mary bore sweet Jesus Christ
> For to redeem us all.

It was over. The chorus filed down from the platform to seats reserved for them.

Bonnie heard little of the rest of the program, as five more choruses, one after another, filled the auditorium with song. She kept wondering: How had Broad Harbor High sounded? Did they have a chance of winning a prize?

The program ended. The judges went out of the room. Bonnie sat on the edge of her chair till they came back. One of them stood up in front of the microphone and looked as if he had an important message. Indeed he had. The trouble was he didn't say it quickly enough. First, he introduced the other judges. Then he told what a difficult task they had been given. All six choruses turned in excellent performances. The judges were extremely gratified to know the high quality of high-school singing in their state. Yet that had made their job harder. They had agreed, however, that two choruses turned in performances slightly better than the others and that one of the two was a shade more perfect than the other. He was, therefore, happy to award first prize to the Billings High School of Rockford and second prize to Bellport's own Jefferson High School chorus.

Happy exclamations rang out. Then the big room was filled with applause. The announcer spoke again.

"Although only two choruses can win the prizes, every boy and girl who sang for us here today receives a five-dollar bill and the hearty thanks of Station WTNZ. And now, the singers are invited to be the station's guests for luncheon. The meal will be served in the gymnasium of the Jefferson High School two blocks down this street. Follow your leaders. Thank you again, young folks."

Bonnie followed the others streaming down the street and into the large, handsome building which was Jefferson High School. She knew now how the football team felt when it lost a game. She tried to avoid Mr. Parker. He must be terribly disappointed in them for not even winning second prize. And in her, the first soprano! Why couldn't she have sung as well as she had at home? The room rang with laughter and merry talk. In it Bonnie was a small island of gravity. She didn't want anything to eat but took a cup of soup onto her tray in the line-up so as not to be conspicuous.

Oh dear! Here was Mr. Parker. He was sitting down beside her. "If he says anything to me, I'll just die," she thought. He only said, "Hi, Bonnie," then spoke to the whole chorus, which sat at a table together. "I'm proud of every one of you. You should have heard the nice things people have been saying about you. Of course I know you were all hoping to bring back a prize, second if not first. Just remember we've been competing with high schools three and four times the size of ours. What's more, if there'd been a third prize we'd have won it. The judges told me so. Next year we'll try again. Next year we'll be seasoned radio performers."

His words cleared the atmosphere like a breeze. Bonnie jumped up. "Guess I'll go and get something more to eat." She came back with a generous serving of ham and potatoes. One or two others went back for more.

Susan was right, thought Bonnie, as they rode home on the bus. It had been silly to daydream about how she would spend that prize money. Five dollars wouldn't buy those wool jackets and the doll for Betty and Ma's handbag.

On Monday afternoon the Bayberry Island girl might have been seen walking into Broad Harbor's largest dry-goods store. Yes, the manager could use an extra girl afternoons, he said, in the toy department. That is, he could use her if she could stay on till the afternoon before Christmas. Could she?

That meant losing four precious vacation days. It meant not getting home till Christmas Eve. She hesitated for only a couple of seconds. "I'll stay." There seemed to be no other way to make sure that Santa Claus found his way to Pretty Cove this year.

18. A White Christmas

BAYBERRY Island, blanketed with snow, looked like a white cloud dropped into the ocean. It was quiet and peaceful and starlit. The firs and spruces alongshore, with wet snow clinging to their branches, bowed in reverent attitudes.

It was Christmas Eve. Bonnie sat in her father's boat and watched the orange-yellow lights shine out from the houses on shore and pictured the people behind those lights busy doing last things for Christmas. She was coming home finally after missing four vacation days. The cheap suitcase at her feet gaped at the corners, it was so full of Christmas. There was a doll carriage that would make Betty's face light up like a Christmas tree. Bonnie could see the little girl dancing all over the house in one of her outbursts of sheer joy. And what would Ma look like when she saw that new handbag — the best-looking one Bonnie could remember her mother owning? There was a new pipe and a can of tobacco for Pa and a big box of candy for the whole family. The jackets for the twins and Betty's doll were already bought with money Bonnie had sent on ahead.

One other present lay tucked away in the suitcase — a handsome blue necktie with small white sailboats and anchors scattered over it — a perfect gift for a boy whose passion was boats. She had never given Jimmy anything for Christmas before. This was a peace offering, with Christmas for an excuse. She planned to give it to him after the entertainment at church tonight if he was there. If not, she would send the necktie over to his house by the twins.

Cranberry Point was a long white finger. And look at the Watson house! It blazed with lights. The family had come back for Christmas just as Greg had said they would.

At the Cove the twins and Betty waited, yelling, "Hi, Bonnie!" As usual their legs looked several inches longer than when she went away. As usual Betty seemed somewhat less little-girlish than the time before. Her light-brown hair no longer lay on her neck in curls. Two little braids stuck out, one from behind each ear, giving her a perky, independent look.

The twins both grabbed the suitcase, eager to carry its precious load. "Got a lot of stuff in there, haven't you?" asked Dave.

"You boys be careful of that. Don't you drop it or it'll burst open."

Betty was at once all suspicion. "You got something in there that'll break?"

"Never you mind."

"I made a present for you, Bonnie — in school, all by myself. You couldn't guess what it is — not in a million trillion years."

The twins giggled. They too had secrets.

"Don't see why Broad Harbor didn't get a prize on the radio," said Billy. "You sang fine. We all listened."

"We didn't get a prize because some of the others sang better."

"We didn't think so."

"I thought you sang a million trillion times better than all the others." This came from Betty.

Yes, it was good to be home.

Ma stood at the kitchen door, framed in light.

Bonnie walked into the warm room that was fragrant with cooking and into her mother's arms. "Seemed like you never would get home this time. My goodness, child! you look worn out."

"I'm all right."

Before they had finished eating supper a bell began to ring out from the Bayberry Island church across the Point. Mrs. Andrews pulled off the apron she had on over her go-to-meeting dress and smoothed her hair before the small looking glass over the sink. "We'll leave the dishes till we get back."

A small procession of Pretty Cove folks were setting out along the footpath for the white box of a church perched on the hill above the harbor. Ma, Bonnie and the twins joined them. Lanterns and flashlights silhouetted their figures against the snow. Their voices mingled with the church bell's ringing, with the whisperings of the trees and the ever-present *swish-swash* of the sea. Bonnie felt wrapped round with warmth and contentment just as the plants were wrapped in the soft blanket of snow. As she looked down onto the village of Bayberry Harbor the words of a Christmas hymn were in her ears:

> O little town of Bethlehem
> How still we see thee lie.

A White Christmas

"Your boy friend's home," announced Billy suddenly. "Saw him at the post office yesterday."

"He asked when you was coming home," contributed Dave.

"When did he get here?" Bonnie tried to keep the eagerness out of her voice.

"Day before yesterday."

"He flew!"

"Flew!" Where did Jimmy get what it cost to fly from Boston?

"His folks flew, too, and they brought a lot of company."

Bonnie was silent. They were talking about Greg — not Jimmy.

"Oh!" and "Ah!" chorused the children when they stepped inside the church and saw the tree, which had been brought from the woods and loaded with bags of candy and trinkets — all for them.

Bonnie wished that Ma and the twins hadn't wanted to sit down front. She couldn't see who was coming in and who was sitting in the back without turning way around. She kept wondering if Jimmy was there. Tonight, Christmas Eve, seemed like a good time to make things up, and the first move, she knew, would have to be hers. Oh, dear! It just wouldn't do to turn her head around again.

159

The program began. The twins and the rest of their Sunday school class were arranging themselves across the platform to sing "Away in a Manger." Not till the formal part of the evening was over and the tree was nearly stripped of its exotic fruit did Bonnie discover Jimmy. He was sitting in the back row, just where he always used to sit. Everyone stood up and sang "O Come, All Ye Faithful." The service was over.

She hurried to the back. At least she tried to hurry, but old friends kept stopping her to wish her Merry Christmas and to make friendly inquiries. At last she was near enough to catch Jimmy's eye. She smiled across an expanse of heads and backs.

"Hi, Jimmy!" Her voice had a singing quality. Here he was, waiting on the steps just the way he used to. He *must* be waiting for *her*.

"Hi, Bonnie!" Something like the old grin seemed to be starting. Then the boy's face stiffened. Gone were even the beginnings of a grin. Quickly he swung around to the girl who was standing beside him. "Come on, Mary," Bonnie heard him say. "Let's go." The girl was Mary Lunt.

"What's your rush, Bonnie?" It was a familiar voice — the voice of Greg Watson. He was right at her elbow. Now she realized that someone had been there saying her name for several seconds. Had

160

A White Christmas

Jimmy seen Greg? Had he thought they were together? Was that why he froze so suddenly? Had he
and Mary come together? Yet Jimmy never used to
have any time for Mary. He said she was dumb.
Bonnie gave up trying to figure it all out.

"Gee! I'm glad you're here," Greg was saying.
"Thought you'd never get here. Isn't Bayberry wonderful with this snow? Just the way Christmas ought
to look. I brought skis. Will you go skiing with me?
Will you come over Sunday for dinner? Mother said
to ask you. Do you think sometimes about the fun we
had on that trip last summer? I do! Why don't I walk
along home with you?"

It was the same Greg, talking as if he were wound
up, ready to fill every minute of her vacation. She was
beginning to feel all out of breath again, just as she
had last summer.

They started down the snowy hill together. A rod
ahead of them walked another couple — Jimmy and
Mary. Bonnie was glad when she and Greg turned off
on the path across Cranberry Point.

"Won't you come in?" she asked halfheartedly.
They stood at the door of her house. Through the
window she could see her father sitting in his socks
in front of the oilstove, listening to the radio. He was
always terribly grumpy with Greg, always acted as if

the boy were nobody he knew or wanted to know. He was even stiffer than Ma, and she acted pretty cool whenever "that good-looking summer boy" came around.

"Can't tonight. Got to get home and help entertain our company. I sort of ran out on them to see you." He pulled a small package out of the pocket of his suède windbreaker. "Got a little something for you. Hope you like it."

"A Christmas present! Oh! Thanks."

"Well, Merry Christmas!" He threw an arm about her and pulled her to him. She felt the leather of his jacket like soft velvet against her chin. There was nothing soft about the kiss he gave her. His lips pressed hard against hers for a few moments, then he was gone, running back along the path, turning once to call back, "Merry Christmas, Bonnie Jean."

The girl stood for several seconds where he left her, like one resting after running very hard. She heard a sloshing sound behind her, then a giggle. Someone seemed to rise right out of the dusky white ground. It was Mabel Collins. She was giggling. Oh, well, Mabel was always giggling. She might not have seen Greg kiss her. It was over so quickly.

"That's the way Mary Lunt gets kissed, I guess. Jimmy's crazy about Mary, I guess."

A White Christmas

Bonnie pretended not to hear a word and went quickly into the house.

"Where's your ma and the kids?" her father wanted to know, surprised to see her come in alone.

"They'll be right along." She went upstairs to her own room. The first thing she did after lighting the oil lamp was to pull the small package out of her coat pocket, tear off silver paper and red ribbon and lift the cover of the cardboard box. "Oh-h-h!" she exclaimed aloud. On a bed of cotton lay a pair of silver earrings, cut in the pattern of snow crystals. She had wanted some earrings for the longest time, and these were utterly beautiful. Standing in front of the looking glass, she screwed them into her ears. They gleamed in the lamplight like two stars. They were no brighter than the girl's eyes.

The next thing Bonnie did was to go to her suitcase, open the lid and rummage till her fingers found a flat box tied with a crisp rosette of tinsel ribbon. How she had fussed over doing up that package! Yanking the rosette apart, she pulled off the wrappings, looked critically at the blue tie with nautical design, then extracted the card inscribed "Merry Christmas from Bonnie to Jimmy" and tore it into pieces no bigger than snowflakes. That tie had been picked out for a blue-eyed boy with a passion for making boats.

Yet it would look well, she decided, on a boy with hazel eyes and a passion for having fun. Hurriedly — before Betty could get home and begin asking questions — Bonnie wrote another card, "Merry Christmas to Greg from Bonnie," slipped it into the box and tied the package up again, but not quite so carefully as it had been tied before.

Betty broke into delighted laughter when she came upstairs and found her older sister already in bed. "You went to bed first!" she crowed. "You got sleepy 'fore I did. I'm not sleepy at all." Bonnie did not open her eyes.

"Oh! look at *you. With earrings on.* Where'd you get 'em? Where *did* you? Did Santa Claus bring 'em already? Tell me, Bonnie. You're not really asleep, are you?"

Bonnie avoided explaining about the earrings, which she had forgotten to take off, by keeping her eyes shut and feigning the soft, regular breathing of a person sound asleep. Yet, long after Betty slept, she lay and looked into the darkness. She lay very still. But she felt out of breath.

"Santa Claus came after all, didn't he? Ma said he might not get here this year 'cause he lost his boat in that big storm." Betty sat on the floor, cradling her new doll and rocking back and forth in an imaginary rocking chair.

Bonnie smiled back at her. "Guess probably he stowed away on the mail boat."

The little girl shouted with delight. "Santa was a stowaway. A stowaway."

Ma said quietly, "Your sister helped him get aboard!"

"You *did?* How'd you do it?"

"Just helped him pop into a big box and Cap'n Taylor thought he was freight."

This simple answer seemed to satisfy the little girl, who went back to rocking the doll and crooning, "Go to sleep, go to sleep, baby."

Mrs. Andrews was transferring change and other small possessions from her worn, old handbag into the glossy new bag. "I'm glad Santa picked out a blue one. I've always had black bags before."

Mr. Andrews sat tipped back in one chair with his feet in another, breaking in the new pipe, which he said was a dandy.

From the yard came the happy voices of the twins, who, warm in their new wool jackets, were rolling up a snowball.

The small spruce tree, which the boys had cut and brought in from the snowy woods, stood in the corner of the room, stripped of everything but a paper star. Every one of the decorations — popcorn strings and candies wrapped in bits of gold and silver paper — had been eaten.

The room was full of small, contented sounds — Betty's soft lullaby, the *puff, puff, puff* of Pa's pipe, the snores of Chummy, made happy by a huge Christmas bone. Even the creaking of the aged rocker which Ma sat in sounded cheerful this afternoon.

19. Expectations

W E wanted so to hear you sing on the radio, Bonnie, but couldn't get that station," said Mrs. Watson. "Won't you sing for us tonight? Sing the song you sang on the great occasion."

It was the Sunday after Christmas. Bonnie had eaten dinner at the house on the Point. Now the Watsons and their house guests and Bonnie were gathered in the living room.

"You mean sing it *alone*?"

"Why not?" asked Greg with a laugh. "If the radio audience didn't scare you, why should we?"

Greg and his mother apparently thought she had sung a solo on WTNZ. "I di . . . " Bonnie began, then stopped. Why tell them all the details? Here was her chance to shine before these people who could do so many things which she couldn't. Why not take it? Why not let them go on being impressed? "All — all right, if you'll come in on the chorus."

Encouraged by their friendliness and their expectations, Bonnie sang better than she ever had before. "Didn't I tell you she had a lovely voice?" asked Greg proudly when she finished the first verse. They all clapped their agreement. Whether they applauded the voice, which was indeed sweet but a bit thin, or the bright-eyed, red-cheeked girl in the red dress herself, none of them probably quite knew.

She went on through the other verses. The holly bark, "as bitter as any gall," held no bitterness here in this pretty room with the Watsons and their friends all clapping and saying nice things. Mrs. Watson clapped hardest and longest. "My child," she exclaimed, "you must have your voice trained! You just can't bury a talent like yours."

A talent like hers! Nobody had ever told her before

168

that she had a talent. Coming from Mrs. Watson, it must mean a lot, the girl thought. She had been to concerts in New York and Boston and heard famous singers.

"And I think I know," Greg's mother went on, "how you can get some training next summer. One of my oldest and best friends teaches voice at the Brandon Music School in New York City. In summer she takes a sort of working vacation at her farm in Massachusetts. Music Hill, she calls it. There she brings together every year for six weeks a few talented young people who can't afford to pay for lessons and are willing to join in a co-operative living plan."

"In working themselves to death," put in Greg.

"Nothing of the kind. They have a wonderful time. Everybody who goes to Music Hill loves it. You'll love it too."

"You really think she'd take me?"

"I certainly do. Alice is a very good friend of mine and I'll write to her tonight and tell her all about you." Mrs. Watson's pretty, childish face was alight with enthusiasm. So far as she was concerned Bonnie's next summer was all settled.

Greg was anything but enthusiastic. "I warn you, Bonnie. You won't like it, no matter what Mother says. They're just a bunch of long-hairs at Music Hill."

"Don't pay the slightest attention to him. Any serious musician is a long-hair to Greg." His mother went on planning her letter to Alice Evans.

As usual, Mr. Watson said little and smiled indulgently on his wife and son.

As for Bonnie, she was in a rapturous state and more out of breath than ever. Go away next summer to a beautiful country place such as Mrs. Watson described and study music! Her imagination pictured her there, applauded and admired just as she had been tonight, off to a fine start on a career as a musician.

"Gosh! Wish I'd never told Mother about your singing on the radio that time." Greg's face was sober as he walked home with her. "She'll fix everything up — she's a dandy little arranger — and you'll spend most of next summer singing *ah-ah-ah-ah* up and down the scale and doing other dopy things instead of having fun with me here on Bayberry. Honest, Bonnie — I'm not kidding — that Evans woman is a driver and she expects everybody who comes there to be a budding genius. You won't like Music Hill."

"You're saying those things because you're so selfish you want me to stay here."

"I'm not either. But gee whizz! I *do* want you to stay here. I'm nuts about you. You're different from any girl I ever knew. Don't you like me better than that boat-building guy? *Don't* you?"

A harsh laugh burst from her lips. "If you mean Jimmy, I don't like him at all, not any more, I don't."

"That's wonderful. Then you . . ."

They had reached the cottage. To Bonnie's surprise the almost never-used front door opened and Ma stood in it. "Hello, Greg," she said. It was the first time she had ever called him by name. "Come in. How would you two like some cookies?"

The girl's eyes bulged in her face. What possessed Ma? Here she was calling "that Watson boy" Greg and inviting him into the house and offering him cookies, which she must have baked specially for the occasion! Then Bonnie remembered something. Mabel must have blabbed about that Christmas Eve kiss. Ma was just trying to head off a second kiss.

Bonnie had decided to be very casual with Jimmy when she saw him again. Just a "Hi, Jimmy" and on her way. Just act barely aware he existed. She never got a chance to put on that little act.

"Jimmy Daniels had a pretty short vacation, didn't he?" remarked Mrs. Collins at the store on Monday as she put evaporated milk into a bag for Bonnie.

"How's that?" asked Bonnie.

"Didn't you know he'd gone back to Boston?"

"Oh, has he?" Bonnie rather overdid that air of neither knowing nor caring where he'd gone or when he'd gone.

"Took the mail boat this morning. Had to get back to his job."

"Oh, yes?"

"My, but he's a hard worker, that boy, and smart as they come." The storekeeper sounded the way Ma did sometimes, as if Bonnie didn't half appreciate Jimmy.

"Mary Lunt seen him off," contributed Mabel with the inevitable giggle.

Bonnie pretended she hadn't heard Mabel. Yet her cheeks gave her away. They burned, but not from the December wind.

"I don't *care*. I don't care what Jimmy does or who does it with him," she insisted all the rest of the day. She kept reminding herself firmly for days that she didn't care about Jimmy.

The girl was actually glad when vacation was over and she went back to Broad Harbor. It would be good to be up to her eyes again in homework, chorus practice, baby-sitting. Life for her on Bayberry Island, once so simple, had grown more complicated than life in town at school.

172

Expectations

"How'd Jimmy like the necktie?" was the first question Susan asked when the two friends sat down to compare Christmases.

"Didn't give it to him. Gave it to Greg Watson."

"To that summer boy? He's not half as nice as Jimmy."

"How do *you* know? You've never even seen Greg."

"I've seen Jimmy. That's enough for me."

"You can have him for all I care, and Greg too. I'm not bothering with boys for a long time. I'm going to be a singer." She told Susan what Mrs. Watson had said about her voice and about going to Music Hill. It sounded too good to come true, she admitted. Yet Mrs. Watson was the kind of person who made things like that happen.

"Oh, Bonnie, maybe you'll sing on radio and television and travel around giving concerts, just like that girl in the movie we saw."

"You never can tell," said the Bayberry Island girl, her dark eyes dreamy.

She confided her hopes to one other person, to Mr. Parker, one day after chorus practice. He looked at her doubtfully. "Bonnie, I don't think you'd be very happy in a place like that, would you?"

"I'd love it," insisted Bonnie.

20. A Door Opens

THE door to Music Hill swung open with unexpected suddenness. Mrs. Watson tackled the matter of Bonnie's musical education at once and with vigor. Early in March a letter came from New York City. The name on the writing paper was Mrs. William Travers Evans. "Dear Miss Andrews," the letter began — *Miss Andrews!*

A Door Opens

My friend Eve Watson has written me all about you. You sound like just the kind of talented girl, who isn't afraid of working hard, we like to hear about and . . .

In short, the lady invited her to be a "member of our Music Hill family" next summer. The wonderful, impossible dream was coming true if — that "if" looked enormous — the folks would let her go.

How would she put it to them? Like this — "I have the most wonderful opportunity. Whether I take it or not will make a difference to my whole life" or more casually, like this — "What would you say, folks, if I went to school next summer? Just heard of a place where . . ."

She rehearsed the scene to herself. She stored up arguments and planned persuasive pleas to batter down their opposition. Lo! When Easter vacation came and she arrived in Pretty Cove, there was no opposition to batter down. It was like getting braced to push open a heavy door only to have it give at a touch and send you reeling backward. The folks at home already knew about Music Hill. Mrs. Watson had written a letter to them, and it must have been a persuasive one, thought Bonnie.

However, it was clear that no one at home felt enthusiastic over the plan. "Your Pa says you can go if you really want to," said Ma in a flat tone of voice.

"Really *want* to? I'm crazy to go."

"You won't like it there. It's way back in the hills."

The girl threw back her head and laughed. "Oh, Ma! I don't care where it is, so long as it's a place I can get to. I'm so happy — so happy!"

Perhaps Bonnie would have been less jubilant if she had heard a brief dialogue which took place between her parents before she came home. It went like this:

MA: Might be a good idea. 'Twould get her away from that Watson boy for six weeks.

PA: That's so.

MA: They're getting too thick.

PA *(With an emphatic nod):* Yep! Tell her she can go.

As for Bonnie, she went singing through that week and came home in June still singing. She had to listen to croaking voices.

"Massachusetts is miles and miles away, isn't it?" Betty kept asking.

Dave grumbled, "Don't see what you want to go off for, right in the middle of the summer."

Billy would back him up with, "What's anybody want to go to school for in the middle of vacation?"

Ma worried about her being "awful homesick."

On the day Bonnie left, four sober-faced people

176

lined up on the dock to see her off. Her own face was full of happy anticipation. Her eyes seemed to reflect the sunlight that sparkled on every ripple in Bayberry Harbor. An impossible dream had been made to come true. She was going to a beautiful country home to study music. Also she was starting out on the longest trip she had ever taken — out of her own state, across another state and into still another.

"Don't forget to change busses at Portland," cautioned Mrs. Andrews. She handed the girl's suitcase over the rail with the solemnity of an undertaker.

Greg and his mother arrived to say good-by. The boy looked as sober as the others did, not at all his breezy self. The only enthusiastic person present besides the traveler was Mrs. Watson. "You'll have a wonderful time and Alice Evans will be awfully nice to you. Don't forget to write us all about it." She had brought magazines and fruit for the journey. Greg said good-by as quickly as possible. Ma and the kids stood and watched the boat get under way and waved hands which seemed too heavy for their arms. Bonnie was glad when their long faces melted into the background of dock, fishhouses and anchored boats.

"Hear you're going up to Massachusetts," remarked Captain Taylor unenthusiastically when he took her fare. "You won't like it there. Gets awful hot in summer. My sister Ella's husband comes from up that way and he says he wouldn't go back if you paid him five times what he gets over to the cannery at Easton."

"How come you have to go to Massachusetts?" put in old Mrs. Barrows from Bayberry Harbor. "Ain't there nobody in Broad Harbor or Easton that can teach music?"

A guest at Whalers' Inn, overhearing these remarks, said she didn't see how anybody could *bear* to leave Bayberry Island in summer.

Bonnie fled forward and sat down behind a pile of boxes and crates. She was sick of hearing people talk as if she needed to have her head examined just because she had grabbed an opportunity to see new places, meet new people and study music, all at the same time. Some folks couldn't understand a girl's having any ambition. She opened one of the magazines Mrs. Watson had given her but could not keep her thoughts on the pages. They went on ahead of the boat.

Once on the bus for Portland, rolling through towns which had never been anything but names to her before, she felt that the summer's adventure had begun.

The driver realized that the dark-eyed girl in the pink dress didn't know her way around very well.

A Door Opens

"I'll see that you get on the right bus," he assured her in reply to anxious questions. "It'll be right across the street from where we stop." When they had arrived in Portland, he even crossed the street with her and put her onto the bus for Elmsford, Massachusetts.

Presently her own state was left behind and she was rolling across New Hampshire. She had expected everything to look somehow different after the bus crossed the state line. Yet the rolling green hills, the woods and the towns all looked about the same. The changes were gradual. Steadily the hills grew higher and the bus climbed steeper grades. Quite suddenly she realized that there were no more blue inlets edging their way up into the green fields and pastures. That *did* seem strange. Early in the afternoon they crossed another line and were in Massachusetts. In a couple of hours she would be at the end of her journey.

"Here's where you get off, you in the pink dress," the driver called. "Somebody going to meet you here?"

Bonnie looked anxiously out at the box of a roadside station labeled "Elmsford." A station wagon stood waiting. MUSIC HILL was painted on its side. "Yes, and they're right here." Immense relief was in her voice.

A young man swung out of the station wagon and came to take her suitcase. He wore only shorts and sneakers. His body was as brown as a lifeguard's at the end of a long season. "Bonnie Jean Andrews? I'm Dan Riker, chauffeur, farmer, general handy man and a few other things at Music Hill. Jump in." He stowed her suitcase under a rear seat and got in beside her.

Bonnie could think of nothing to say to this man, who must be ten years older than she. Fortunately, Dan was quite ready to do the talking. "I hear you live in a lighthouse out in the ocean."

"I live in a house on dry land, like anybody else."

He laughed. "I'll try again. You live on a rocky little island and this is the first time you've ever been on the mainland."

Where had he got hold of such ideas? What *had* Mrs. Watson written about her?

"Bayberry Island is rocky but it's not all rocks, and I've been going to high school on the mainland for three years."

"Well, well. Here I've been picturing you perched on a rock with the sea gulls, just a child of nature."

Bonnie changed the subject from herself to the man at the wheel.

"Are you a musician?" she asked bluntly.

"I'm not one of Mrs. Evans's hand-picked, guaran-

teed geniuses, if that's what you mean. But I like
music and I teach it in the schools of New Hampton,
Mass."

What did he *mean* — "hand-picked, guaranteed
geniuses"? Was she supposed to be a *genius?*

"Oh! A teacher." No wonder he had seemed grown
up.

"Don't be awed. I shan't be teaching you. I'm just
a handy man at Music Hill. My only pupils in summer
are the gals at a camp over on Lake Killicut. At present I'm coaching them for a concert which will knock
Elmsford cold — I hope. And now, my little sea gull,
we are ascending Music Hill. The big white house up
there will be your home for six weeks and the rather
chesty, well-fed lady on the porch, dressed in white,
is Mrs. William Travers Evans, who will be telling you
in a minute that she wants you to feel like one of the
family."

21. "Different from Living
on an Island"

THE lady in white on the porch stood up to her full five feet nine inches. The Bayberry Island girl walked up the steps, feeling like a small skiff approaching a seventy-five-foot dragger.

"Welcome to Music Hill. So you're Eve Watson's little friend." Mrs. Evans extended her hand and smiled down on Bonnie. "You should read all the nice things she wrote me about you. I hope you'll feel at home and be very happy with us."

"I — I guess I will. It's so beautiful here."

"We think it is, but of course you'll find it very different from living on an island. And now I'll show you where your room is." She led off into the house and up two flights of stairs to a small room with two couches, two desks, two bureaus and two chairs in it.

A tall, blond girl with wide blue-gray eyes sat at one of the desks. She was, it seemed to Bonnie, as beautiful as a movie star. "Mary Lou, this is the girl I've been telling you about — Bonnie Jean Andrews," introduced Mrs. Evans. "Bonnie, this is Mary Lou Berger, your roommate. I'll just leave you two to get acquainted." The lady sailed away. She was more like an ocean liner than a dragger, the island girl decided.

"Pretty imposing, isn't she?" said Mary Lou, reading the other girl's thoughts, "but she's human when you get to know her. Really she is."

"I guess it takes a long time to know her." A small sigh accompanied the remark.

"Don't worry. She's awfully interested in you. So long now. It's my turn to help get supper. I'll be back and take you down."

So Mrs. Evans was "awfully interested" in her. She

183

tried to guess what Mrs. Watson had written. Something about a poor little girl she had discovered living on an island far away from everything, who had sung on the radio? Did the lady expect her to be one of those "guaranteed geniuses"?

Bonnie went to work unpacking her suitcase and the parcel she had sent on ahead by mail. She had just finished cleaning up and putting her things away when the jingle of an old-fashioned string of sleigh bells sounded downstairs. Mary Lou came running in breathlessly. "Suppertime. We'd better go right away. Mrs. Evans never sits down till we're all there."

The meal was served at a long table in a kind of glorified woodshed. The old beams had been scrubbed and painted with linseed oil. The floor was paved with flat stones like a terrace. The furniture was antique and valuable.

She found herself seated beside a man introduced as Mr. Evans, who was so quiet he seemed almost like part of the furniture. Having asked her if she had a comfortable trip, he seemed to consider his duty done. The dark, silent young woman on her left was Ernestine Mannheimer. Bonnie tried to think of something to say to those two but didn't succeed. Then she discovered that it was not necessary for her to talk at all unless someone asked her a question. Conversa-

tion flowed from the head of the table in a stream, as
from a fountain, the fountainhead being Mrs. Evans.
Occasionally someone else made a few remarks. The
talk was almost entirely of music, especially the piano
recital they had attended the night before. Bonnie
had never heard of the pianist. The composers mentioned were unknown to her. Her table companions
might as well have been speaking Siamese for all she
got out of the conversation.

She felt herself shrinking in size, like Alice in Wonderland after taking one of those doses that made her
grow smaller and smaller. She was younger than any
of the others and — she had to admit — compared to
them knew precious little about music. She began
studying them. On one side of Mrs. Evans sat Mary
Lou, beautiful and poised, as poised as a woman of
thirty, though she couldn't be much over twenty. On
the other side was Tony — Tony Arenzi, who flashed
a wonderful smile and laughed easily, as though his
laughter was always ready to be uncorked. Rose
Arenzi had a quieter air and didn't look at all like her
brother, if he was her brother. Any laughter in the
girl Ernestine must be buried deep down, thought
Bonnie. Bonnie stole sideways looks at her. Those
dark eyes were like wells sunk in the white face.
When she smiled one of her rare smiles she looked

185

like a girl. When she sat deep in thought her face turned into an old woman's face. What would make a girl look like that? she wondered.

Dan Riker, who sat across from her, seemed more subdued than he had on the way from the bus station. Yet he talked more than any of the rest except Mrs. Evans and seemed to know more about music and musicians than they. Dan, she soon realized, had the advantage of being an old-timer at Music Hill. He had spent five seasons there. Yet he was not the *top* favorite. That was Tony. Bonnie could see that Mrs. Evans was especially keen about Tony. Each of these five young people was different from anyone else she had ever met before.

"Mrs. Evans says you've sung on the radio." That was the first thing Mary Lou said when, several hours later, they were alone together in their room. She sounded impressed.

"Yes, I did. It was a contest. Our high school chorus and five others took part."

"Oh! You sang in a chorus? I thought Mrs. Evans said . . . "

"I sang in the quartet. I was the first soprano," put in Bonnie quickly and wished to heaven she had never let the Watsons think she had performed alone.

"What station were you on?"

186

"Different from Living on an Island"

"WTNZ."

"Oh! Where's that?"

"In Bellport."

"Oh! Where's that?"

She was shrinking again. Those "Oh's" were certainly deflating.

"Bellport is quite a large city and it's about a hundred miles from Broad Harbor, where I go to school."

To Bonnie's relief her roommate stopped asking questions. Presently she began to answer some of Bonnie's. Ernestine, the girl with the deep-set eyes, was a DP. She had lived through a year in one of Hitler's concentration camps. When the Americans found her she was alive and that was all. She was much younger than she looked — only twenty-one. Her voice was wonderful — a very high coloratura. She would be another Lily Pons some day. So Mrs. Evans said. Tony would be famous, too. He had a tenor like Tagliavini's. Already he sang in a New York City church. Yes, he had been born in New York and grew up there. He was one of Mrs. Evans's pets. Rose wasn't his sister. She was his wife and a fine pianist. She always accompanied him when he gave a recital. Dan was a kind of fixture. He could do just about any job around the place and Mrs. Evans couldn't get along without him and knew it. He divided his time between Music Hill and a girls' camp at the lake, where he taught music. "He's engaged to the head of the camp. That's one reason why he comes here." Mr. Evans was around only for week ends and never had much to say to anybody. "There, I guess I've given you the low-down on everybody."

"You haven't told me about Mary Lou Berger."

"Oh, I'm not a long-hair like the others," laughed Mary Lou. "I sing in a supper club at home — home is Indianapolis — and I want to be a second Hildegarde, or rather a Margot. Margot is my professional name."

"I should think any girl as beautiful as you could do anything she wanted to," said Bonnie frankly and fervently, thereby winning a warm friend.

"It takes a voice and training too, if you want to make the big cities."

"Everybody here is a second somebody or other," thought Bonnie, "everybody except me." It seemed that they were all on the way to being famous.

"You won't find much time for fun here," warned the roommate. She seemed to be afraid this seventeen-year-old might have come to Music Hill for a good time. "Mrs. Evans expects us to practice, practice, practice, and in between times to listen to lectures or help in the house or with the work outdoors. Her

188

idea of an evening of fun is for us to sing together or listen to recordings of great musicians. We all work awfully hard."

"I'm used to working hard. I work hard at home."

"Then you'll feel right at home here."

Bonnie wasn't so sure about that. At the moment Music Hill seemed a bewildering place full of people who knew a tremendous lot and looked upon her as a kind of curiosity. Nothing was the way she had pictured it, least of all Mrs. Watson's old friend, Mrs. Evans, who scared her to death.

22. The Tryout

"I F you love music you will love this place." It was Ernestine Mannheimer speaking, saying each word carefully and with a pronounced accent. "Never did I expect to be so happy again as I have been here." The German girl looked as if she might burst forth singing. She was showing "the new girl" around the place at Mrs. Evans's request and doing it with the zeal of a religious missionary.

They entered a large red barn. "*Ah-ah-ah-ah-ah-ah-ah,*" floated down in a tenor voice from where a haymow had once been. "That is Tony. Hasn't he a beautiful voice? He will be one of the great ones some day." She showed how the place had been divided into practice rooms, each with a number on the door, and how the partitions could be pushed up and into the walls to turn it back into one big hall. "Every Saturday night we have some kind of concert or recital here."

"This we call Cadenza Cottage." Ernestine pointed to a little house in a grove of white birches a short distance from the barn. "A person who needs to practice alone can do it there and not be disturbed by anyone else's trills. That's Rose you hear playing."

"And now," said the German girl when she had showed Bonnie all the buildings, the garden and a small swimming pool, "I shall show you the best-of-all place — the chapel in the woods, we call it." The two entered a pine woods.

Ernestine led the way along a path into a wide glade that was like a brown-needle-floored room in the middle of the woods, walled by the trunks of trees, roofed by the sky. "It's like Secret Cove," thought Bonnie. Yet it wasn't like Secret Cove at all except for the feeling it gave her — that sense of apartness and of peace.

"I come here when I just have to be alone," said

Ernestine. "Sometimes we have music here, and on Sundays a little service."

She, too, would seek this place when she just had to be alone, Bonnie decided.

They came out of the woods onto a grassy hilltop. "Here are the mountains. That tallest one that looks all rocks is Stark Mountain." She named the others. The island girl looked out across the fields to a wall of blue hills. It was a beautiful view. Yet she found herself instinctively looking for a break in that wall and had to remind herself that the sea was not out beyond the horizon but miles away.

Skirting a hayfield, the two girls came to a vegetable garden and to Bonnie's morning work assignment. Bonnie had told Mrs. Evans, when given a choice of jobs, that she would like to work outdoors. "Here's a new helper for you, Dan," said Ernestine. "Mrs. Evans told me to leave Bonnie with you."

Dan Riker, squatted between two rows of onions, looked doubtfully at the island girl and asked of the other, "Does she know an onion from a weed?"

"Suppose you ask her. *Auf Wiedersehen.*"

Bonnie did not wait for the question. "I sure do, and a beet from a turnip and young corn from grass and eelgrass from . . ."

"Stop! Stop! You know more than I do. Go to it."

He looked at Ernestine's retreating back for a few moments, then asked, "Have you heard her sing yet?"

"No."

"She's wonderful." His glance seemed to descend from a height to the girl beside him. "You take those two rows."

They worked in silence for a minute, then Dan began to talk, this time about himself — how he had been coming here for five summers, partly because he could get a summer in the country and pay his expenses by chauffeuring and gardening and partly because the lectures in music history and music appreciation counted toward the degree he was working for. "Mrs. Evans would have a job finding anyone else who could do all the things I can," he bragged. Then his manner changed suddenly. "Once upon a time when Dan was sweet sixteen like you . . . "

"Seventeen," Bonnie corrected him quickly.

"O.K. Make it seventeen. Anyway, I thought in those days that I was going to be a great singer. So did my father and mother. *They* were sure of it. But I was kidding myself. My voice, I found out, was slightly above the average. That was all. So now I try to make singers out of other guys. And — to tell the truth — I love it. When do you have your tryout with Mrs. Evans?" he asked.

"My *what?*"

"Your tryout. She'll have you into her music room and make you stand up and sing scales over and over. Then she'll tell you what she thinks of your voice, and she *will* tell you, believe me."

"She wants to see me at nine tomorrow."

"That'll be *it.*"

"When do you sing for Mrs. Evans?" asked Mary Lou that night when the girls were in their room. It was evidently a turning point in one's life — that first appearance in the room with the baby grand piano and the big, flat-topped desk. Those couldn't be butterfly wings beating inside her stomach. Butterfly wings were too fragile to make such a commotion.

"*Ah-ah-ah-ah-ah-ah-ah,*" began Bonnie as Mrs. Evans gave her the pitch on the piano.

"Try again. A girl who has sung on the radio must have more voice than that . . .

"Again . . .

"See if you can fill this room. Relax your throat . . .

"Give me some full, round tones . . .

"I want to hear you perfectly from in here." She had opened the double doors into the large living room and was standing at the farther end.

194

The Tryout

"I could hardly hear you. Now, again."

How could she relax? How could she produce full, round tones? How could she sing another note? This was not at all what Bonnie had expected. She had pictured herself standing up and singing some familiar song. Instead she had to sing *Ah* up and down the scale. She had expected smiling interest, not head-shakings and repeated demands to "try again." Nothing in her past had prepared her for this. She was not doing herself justice. Yet her best would not have been good enough for this woman, who was looking for "guaranteed geniuses." She knew that now.

"That will do. Sit down, please." Mrs. Evans patted a place on the sofa beside her. Bonnie sat down, but as far to the other end of the seat as possible.

"I think I ought to tell you frankly that you have a light voice, a rather little voice, and that you use it badly. It is sweet and you have an excellent ear for music, but I would not be playing fair with you if I encouraged you, as Eve Watson evidently did, to think that you could have a career as a singer. Eve is an enthusiast. She simply loves to 'discover' people and 'bring them out.' She has a kind heart but very little common sense."

That seemed to dispose of Mrs. Watson, also of herself. Bonnie waited in miserable silence for Mrs.

Evans to say that the Portland bus left at seven in the morning and that Dan would drive her to the station. How could she ever go back and face Bayberry Island?

The lady beside her talked on. "With your ear for music and your love of it you can get a great deal out of six weeks here. I can help you start learning how to use your voice. And I can expose you to some great music. Now it's time for Tony's lesson."

So she wasn't going to be sent home. That was something.

Bonnie went straight to the pine woods, just as she used to head for Secret Cove when life got tough at home. Parting the branches, she went along the path, entered the cool outdoor room, and threw herself down on the brown needles. Tears, held back for an hour, ran down her cheeks. Gradually the lump in her throat melted and the tenseness of her body eased. She turned over and looked up into the sky and did some thinking.

Here were the hard facts. Mrs. Watson in one of her bursts of enthusiasm had arranged for her to come to a place where she didn't really belong. Her "great adventure" was turning into a rather silly little adventure, her voice into "a rather little voice." She could stay and study in this bewildering place among

196

these talented young people or she could go home.

Go home? After everybody on the island knew about Bonnie's great opportunity to study music. Go home? Nothing could be worse. She would stay and take it, stay and get what she could from this place.

Yet even as the girl made this resolve, homesickness, held in check till now, swept over her with the force of a ten-foot wave. The longing for Pretty Cove was like a pain deep down inside of her.

"Excuse me. I did not know anybody was here." It was Ernestine Mannheimer. She started to retreat, then caught a full view of the island girl's face and changed her mind. "Something has made you very unhappy."

"Yes."

"Was it Mrs. Evans?"

"She said I had a light voice, a small voice." Bonnie winked fast. She hoped the light in here was too dim to show that her eyes were brimming. "She said that the lady who wrote her about me didn't have any common sense. She said . . ." Oh, dear, she was all choked up again.

The other was tactful enough to look straight ahead into the woods. "You mustn't take Mrs. Evans too hard. She always bears down on the newcomers. She wants us all to be little budding prima donnas, but of course we can't be. Then too, she's terribly afraid somebody will come here just for a good time. Last summer she pronounced Mary Lou as 'not the Music Hill type.' Now she says the girl has a real future in popular music. She called Dan a 'routine musician,' when he first came. Now he's a 'future force in education.'"

It was kind of Ernestine to talk like this. Yet Bonnie knew in her heart that Mrs. Evans had told the truth. She had been indulging herself in a daydream. No one but the enthusiastic Mrs. Watson ever thought she had a voice out of the ordinary. Mr. Parker at school never said so. He chose her for the quartet on the radio because her voice was higher than the other sopranos'. She remembered how surprised he had looked when she told him about going to Music Hill and how he had said he didn't think she'd be happy there.

"What did Mrs. Evans call Tony?" asked Bonnie.

"Oh, Tony's different. He's one of her own discoveries. She'll tell you how she heard him singing in his father's fruit store in New York and said, 'That boy has a voice in a million,' and walked right into the store and invited him to come to Music Hill."

"And you?"

The German girl flushed self-consciously. "I was

lucky. She took a fancy to my voice. Maybe it was because she felt sorry for me. I was terribly unhappy when I came. A displaced person, they called me, and that was what I felt like."

A bell rang across the fields. "It's time for my lesson. I must go. Please do not be unhappy. You are too young and pretty for that. If you only knew what you have — a home, your family alive and with you and your own country, the one you were born in. You have *everything*."

You have everything. Bonnie repeated the words. Why, that was true. Compared with this lonely young woman with no home, no family, no country, she did have everything that mattered.

23. Many Discoveries

IT's all over, Bonnie. There isn't any more."

The girl came back with a start to Massachusetts, to Elmsford, to the concert hall. Everyone was getting up and leaving, while she still sat in her seat. The sound of a great sea was in her ears, and wind roaring through a forest. She had breasted mighty tides and come out into calm, sunlit seas only to go through another storm. That composer Sibelius must have heard all the sounds she knew so well. He had steered a boat too — through terrible storms — and reached port.

Bonnie said almost nothing as Dan drove the Music

Hill family home from the concert. She heard nothing the others said. An orchestra still played to her. She had just been to her first symphony concert. For the past three weeks the island girl had been discovering something like a new world. She had glimpsed it first in the music room at the house, listening to records of great singers, pianists, violinists and orchestras. Then a very fine violinist — a friend of Mrs. Evans — had come and played at Music Hill. His music had cast a spell over her, making her want to dance with joy and then to sob.

This concert tonight came as a climax to the past weeks. It had taken her to far places. It had taken her home. It had almost torn her apart, then given her peace — *such peace*. Records of symphony orchestras heard at school and at Music Hill had not prepared her for the reality.

No longer did Bonnie feel small. Instead she felt part of something big.

Here at Music Hill she looked far out, away from her island, from the Maine coast, even from her own country, not only into the world of music but into the lives of people who had lived entirely differently from herself.

"I'd never seen green fields like these till two years ago," Tony said casually one day.

"You'd *never seen green fields?*" This didn't seem possible.

"The only grass I'd ever put my feet on was in the parks, when the cops didn't see me and chase me off."

He talked about a childhood played out in paved schoolyards and paved streets, when played at all. Most of the time after school he had worked in his father's fruit store. Amazed, Bonnie listened to his description of a school with ten times as many boys and girls as there were at Broad Harbor High and to stories of fights between the boys of his street and a gang of "tough guys from downtown." Those stories were right out of the movies.

Tony told her, too, of another side of life in New York City. Fine concerts in parks and museums absolutely free. Paintings brought from all over the world, which one could see without paying a cent. Evening classes in just about anything one could want to study.

Mary Lou's world was almost as different from her own, and from Tony's, too, as life on another planet. She had grown up on a wide, fertile farm, where she looked out on waves of corn and wheat stretching as far as she could see. No hills, no rocks, no sea — just level fields to the horizon. It was a two-hundred-acre farm. The Maine girl had difficulty picturing a farm as big as that.

Many Discoveries

The Midwestern girl's life was different in another way. She had always known security — not wealth, but a good comfortable home life, where a girl never had to wonder whether she could have a new coat or would have to make do with a worn old one or whether or not she could buy anybody a Christmas present.

Dan, as Bonnie helped him in the garden and about the place, talked of life in a small manufacturing city and of his own rebellion against monotonous work in a textile factory. He resolved that he was not going to feed a machine all his life. Because he had a pleasant tenor and sang Sundays in a church choir and got paid for it, and because the minister and all his friends said so much about his voice, Dan dreamed of becoming a professional singer. Like Bonnie, he at her age had thought it would be a fairly simple matter. He had gone to Boston and worked his way while he studied at the Conservatory of Music. "Of course I soon learned that I didn't have what it takes to be a singer," the young man confided. "So I studied to be a teacher. Now I'm doggoned glad it turned out that way. Life isn't much fun if you have to be thinking about your voice and taking care of your precious little throat and practicing all the time. Look at Ernestine. Look at Tony. They'd rather sing than eat.

They don't care about anything in the world as much as they do about music. I couldn't ever be like that. Besides, I like to do things with other people, not just by myself."

"So do I," agreed Bonnie. She realized now that being a professional singer was a far more complicated business than she had supposed, also a bit lonely.

"At your age," Dan said to her one day, "I went at things wrong end to, like you have."

"What do you *mean* — wrong end to?" For a moment she thought he was criticizing the way she was thinning the carrots.

"Instead of doing something just because I loved to do it, I wanted most of all to make a great big name for a little guy called Dan."

The girl stood still and stared across the green fields. Why, Dan was *right!* She *had* been like that. In the school play, in the school chorus and up here too, always her first thought had been of proving that Bonnie, "the little island girl," was *somebody* very important. It suddenly seemed pretty childish and, as Dan had said, entirely "wrong end to."

Rose and Ernestine took the island girl into other countries. Rose showed her life in an Italian village — as simple and friendly as on Bayberry Island. That is, her village had been like that before the great bombers flew over it. She told what it had been like to come to America as a bride.

With Ernestine, Bonnie went into a happy, pre-Hitler, prewar home in Berlin. As the German girl talked, the other realized that this home was not very different from an American home except that the mother and father and children spoke a different language.

Ernestine never told what happened to that family when a wild storm of hatred raged across the land and struck that home. She always stopped her story abruptly. Mrs. Evans and Mary Lou supplied the grim details. Yet without these details, Bonnie would have known that this girl had lived in darkness and without hope, through terrors of which she could not speak. All this was recorded in her eyes, in cheeks that seemed permanently hollowed, in a voice vibrant with feeling.

So it was that the island girl made still another discovery — that freedom could be snatched away from a whole people overnight.

No longer did the hills along the sky seem to shut her in. All the time her horizon was pushed back farther and farther.

Homesickness seldom bothered her now. She had

also discovered several ways of curing it. One was to read or reread a letter from home. Ma relied mostly on postal cards, but it was remarkable how much she could crowd into a few inches of space — that lobsters were shedding their shells, how Pa and the Joyces had gone tuna-fishing together and speared a five-hundred-pounder, that she had put up ten quarts of raspberries and cut out and basted Bonnie's new plaid woolen dress.

The twins painfully produced a letter between them. Nothing could have been a more convincing proof of their affection than this blotted, misspelled, much worked-over note, with words crossed through and rewritten. At the end was a postscript laboriously printed by Betty. It read:

BUTTERBALL HAS FOUR KITTENS. CHUMMY AND THE WATSON DOG HAD A FIGHT. LOVE FROM BETTY

Bonnie carried that note around in her sweater pocket and read and reread it till the paper went to pieces.

Mrs. Watson wrote, too. Her letter was full of enthusiasm about Bonnie's future and "best wishes for all sorts of good luck." Greg wrote often and kept saying he missed her. He also wanted her to be sure to get home in time for another cruise on the *Summer Wind* the third week in August. She must come. It would be a reunion of last year's gang.

Nobody ever mentioned Jimmy. Yet surely he must come home sometimes, for he was back working at Easton. He had a man-sized job at the boatshop now.

One evening, when the others had gone to the village to do errands and she was alone in the house, Bonnie turned on the big radio in the living room. She twiddled the pointer from side to side, first far to the left then far to the right, having no idea where to get the local stations. Suddenly, to her amazed delight, the room was filled with those familiar cackle-like voices: fishermen calling from their boats up and down the coast. It was like being home again! Pulling her chair close to the radio, she listened for the name of some boat she knew, the *Ellen D.* from Pretty Cove or the *Betty Jo* from Bayberry Harbor or the big *Sea Rover* from Easton. Instead she heard the *Sea Wind* calling off Highland Light, Cape Cod, and the *Lizzie Allen* reporting that she was coming into Gloucester with a load of mackerel. All strange boats, calling from strange waters.

"Heavens! what a frightful racket. You've got the

short wave on. Let me show you where to get the local stations."

Mrs. Evans had come home. She gave a quick twist to the knob and the music of a symphony orchestra floated into the room. To Bonnie the "frightful racket" had been a symphony — a fisherman's symphony. She resolved to listen to it again another time when she found herself alone with the radio. There was always a chance of hearing familiar names, even familiar voices.

24. The *Cormorant* Calling

Nor till the last week of her stay did Bonnie
have a chance to listen again for the fishermen. In fact she was not thinking much about fishermen or Bayberry Island or even Pretty Cove these
days. She had become part of the busy Music Hill
life and every day was full.

She practiced scales, and listened to lectures. She
picked vegetables, picked and arranged flowers,
sprayed rosebushes, raked the lawn. She took in her
stride weekly criticisms from the stately head of

Music Hill. Mrs. Evans even handed her a compli-
ment now and then, such as, "You have an excellent
ear," or, "Your music memory is exceptional."

Busier than any of the other four were the last two
weeks. Rehearsals began for the final recital and
everybody had something to do. Ernestine and Tony
practiced solos. Rose practiced accompaniments, also
a piano solo. All six rehearsed madrigals and folk
songs together, with Dan both singing and directing.

Excitement ran high as August days shortened,
especially among those who had leading parts. A well-
known radio tenor, a friend of Mrs. Evans's would be
there. The whole summer colony — including a singer
in the Metropolitan Opera company — would turn
out. Bonnie felt the way she imagined the man who
played the triangle and the timpani in an orchestra
might feel — a tiny part of something important.

One evening a few days before the big event she
found herself alone once more in the living room.
Again she turned on the radio at the short-wave end.
Again the voices of fishermen filled the room. Perhaps
this time she would hear from home waters, from a
home boat. Yet, as before, the names of men, and
boats, and places were all unfamiliar. She was just
about to turn the pointer to a local station when an
SOS came through.

The Cormorant *Calling*

The Cormorant *calling.*

The Cormorant *on fire ten miles southwest Seal Rock Light.*

Seal Rock Light! That was home. It was beyond Long Island. A boat on fire way out there!

The *Cormorant*. The *Cormorant*, she repeated. It was no Bayberry Island boat. Yet somehow the name had a familiar ring. Where had she heard it? Where *had* she?

The voice went on calling the Coast Guard. It sounded more and more desperate. Would nobody answer? There was something familiar about the voice, too, in spite of the cracked unnaturalness of the tone.

Suddenly Bonnie remembered something and her heart gave a great thump against her chest. The *Cormorant* was one of Fred Murphy's boats. She had heard Jimmy speak of going out on it! Jimmy was on the *Cormorant* tonight! She *knew* it. He was calling out of the darkness for help. Would *nobody* answer? She could only sit here miles away and listen.

It seemed a half hour, though it was really only a few minutes, before the Coast Guard picket boat answered. She heard the man asking for the *Cormorant's* exact location and Jimmy telling him. His voice sounded agonized now. Then nothing more.

Only the voices of strangers from strange boats came through.

Mary Lou and Dan, coming in much later, found Bonnie sitting rigid, frozen to the edge of the chair, listening to squawking voices and staring into space as though she saw a terrible sight. Her white face seemed all eyes.

"Don't turn it off! Don't turn it off!" she shrieked when Mary Lou started to shut off the radio.

They thought she was sick and delirious — this staring girl who talked incoherently about a cormorant and Jimmy and a fire. Finally, above the noise of the radio, they pieced together the story of what had happened — that the *Cormorant* was a boat, not a bird; who Jimmy was and where he was. They were relieved when the Bayberry Island girl began to cry. Anything was better than that frozen look.

Dan, the practical, had an idea. "We'll find out. We'll telephone to the mainland town nearest that rock. What is it? The operator'll know if there's been a bad fire, if anybody's hurt."

Bonnie stopped sobbing and told him to call Broad Harbor.

He went at once to the telephone, asked for the Broad Harbor, Maine, operator and told the story.

Did she know what had happened? It was desperately important for him to find out. The operator said she would call him back.

Ten minutes. Twenty minutes. They sat and waited for the call, while those cracked voices came over the radio. Bonnie still listened to them, hoping that she might hear something directly from the *Cormorant*. Dan was about to call Broad Harbor again when the bell rang. He ran to answer before Bonnie could get there, but she stood right at his elbow, listening to his side of the conversation and watching his face.

"Yes? . . . There was? . . . A young man and two boys? Do you know their names? . . . You don't? They're in Broad Harbor Hospital? Will you call the hospital? . . . Yes. I'll hang up."

They waited again, this time for ten minutes. Then the operator reported that the line was busy but she would call him as soon as she could get the hospital.

Twenty minutes.

"The line is still busy," said the operator.

"Keep ringing them," Dan told her.

They tried to play a game of canasta. That is, Mary Lou and Dan did. Yet their minds were not on the game. Like Bonnie, they listened all the time for the telephone to ring. And all the time they were con-

213

scious of a small, tense figure and a pair of dark eyes fixed on something three hundred miles away. When at last the call came through, Bonnie got to the telephone before anyone else could. Mary Lou and Dan stood beside her and listened.

"Yes. Yes. What are their names? . . . Robert Murphy, Harold Murphy and James Daniels." She repeated the names.

"On the critical list? One of them? *Which* one?" There was silence. Then the receiver fell out of Bonnie's hand and clattered onto the table.

The other two began to talk. Nobody could tell a thing from what they gave out at a hospital. Being on the critical list might mean anything. That hospital operator didn't know how he really was. In the morning they would call the nurse who was taking care of Jimmy. It was wasted breath. Bonnie did not hear a word. She wasn't there. Mary Lou and Dan were relieved when Mrs. Evans came in and took charge of this girl who neither saw nor heard them and who sat and shivered though the August night was warm.

Mrs. Evans gave Bonnie a hot drink and put her to bed in her own room. The first thing the girl said was, "I'll have to go home tomorrow." She was sorry to leave before the recital but she simply *had* to go to see how Jimmy was. Could Dan take her to the seven o'clock bus in the morning?

"Of course he can, dear. But if I were you I wouldn't try to make any plans tonight. First thing in the morning we'll call up the hospital. We may find then that your friend is in no danger. Now you'd better go to sleep."

Instead of going to sleep, Bonnie got up, went upstairs to her own room and packed her suitcase. Instead of going to sleep, she lay and wondered if Jimmy was terribly burned. She could see him all swathed in bandages, or half-drowned. Were they using a pulmotor on him, trying to bring him to? Sleeping was worse than lying awake. She dreamed of being out in the *Water Spider* with Jimmy. Great waves towered above them. Then one wave, as long and dark as Stark Mountain, rushed toward them. But it wasn't a wave. The mountain was falling on top of them. "Help! Help! Help for the *Water Spider*," she shrieked.

"Can't you eat something before you start?"

"I just couldn't, Mrs. Evans."

"Well, Dan's all ready and here are some sandwiches for your lunch. Hadn't you better take some extra money?"

215

"Thank you. I've got plenty." Her plenty consisted of her return bus ticket and a ten-dollar bill, which had lain in her handbag unbroken all these weeks, saved for an emergency.

It was six-thirty. Bonnie, though dressed in the same cotton dress she had worn the night before, looked too small for it this morning. Her face beneath the pink kerchief tied over her hair looked thinner than the same face did yesterday. She had been up since five o'clock in her anxiety not to miss the bus.

"Good-by, Bonnie." To the girl's surprise, Mrs. Evans kissed her. "Be sure and let me hear from you."

"Good-by. I will. Tell the others good-by for me."

It was over. The car started rolling down the hill road. Thank heaven, the others still slept. One more good-by and she would have blubbered and made an awful fool of herself. It wouldn't take much to set her off this morning. How wonderful they had all been! She wished she could tell them so but she couldn't talk. Dan — blessings on him — kept his eyes fixed on the road and said nothing.

They came at last to the roadside bus station. Dan stood with her in front of the three-sided box and waited, still not talking. Neither said anything until the bus came along. Then the young man said quickly as he handed up her suitcase, "Good-by, Bonnie. Good luck. Thanks for all the help you gave me in the garden."

Some day she would thank him for standing by and understanding. She couldn't thank anybody for anything now. Five words repeated themselves over and over in her ears, the words that had come over the telephone this morning — *Still on the danger list.* James Daniels was still on the danger list. That was all she could find out and all she could think of.

The hills dropped down behind the bus. Quickly the landscape began to level off, but none too quickly for the dark-eyed girl in a pink dress with a pink kerchief over her head. She kept looking for a point or scallop of blue cutting into the green fields and rocky pastures, for a bit of sea pushing up into a sluggish stream and giving it life, for sea gulls and terns. When she could glimpse any of these things, then home would not seem so far away.

Yet even as Bonnie wished the miles away she began to dread the journey's end at the hospital and the question she had to ask, "How is James Daniels?"

She turned her thoughts forcefully backward — to Music Hill. Her great adventure was over. At first she had been disappointed and called it a little adventure. Yet now she knew it had truly been a great adventure. At first she had felt deflated, shrunk in size and importance. Quite suddenly she realized that she had grown. This Bonnie Andrews was a bigger person than the girl who set out in June, less self-important but much bigger. Once her world had been an island, or rather a group of islands. Then it had grown to include Broad Harbor and a little strip of mainland. Now her world covered hundreds of miles. It was not even confined to one country.

A smell told her first that she was near the coast — the smell of seaweed. Then there were white wings in the sky reflecting the sunlight, the wings of sea gulls. Something Jimmy once said came back to her, "I belong here. No matter where I go I'll always come back to Bayberry Island."

"And so will I," said Bonnie out loud — to the surprise of the woman who shared the seat with her.

25. "An Even Chance"

WHAT was the matter with her legs? Bonnie could hardly force them up the steps of Broad Harbor Hospital. She had to push them with all her strength to the information desk in the bare hall.

The woman who sat behind the desk wore a stiff white dress and a stiff little cap. She turned cool blue eyes on Bonnie. "James Daniels?" she repeated, then turned to a typewritten list. "Jimmy is just a name on the list to her," thought the girl.

"His condition is unchanged."

"You mean he's still in danger?"

"His name is still on the critical list."

"Is that all you can tell me?"

"I'm afraid it is."

"I'd like to see him, please." She tried to sound as cool as the nurse but couldn't keep a little tremble out of her voice.

"Are you a member of his family?"

Bonnie shook her head.

"No one but his family is allowed to see him." The woman behind the desk looked into the face lifted to hers. She was used to seeing anxious faces. Those were almost the only kinds she did see. Yet this face beneath the bright kerchief was so young — too young to look so tortured. "Suppose you go up and see Miss Sims. She's the nurse in charge of the ward he's in. Take the elevator to the third floor, turn right and go to the end of the corridor."

Bonnie took the elevator, turned right and walked past one room after another. Through the open doors she glimpsed white beds, each with an unnaturally quiet figure under an immaculate cover. Some were propped up and aware of everything that went on.

"An Even Chance"

Others lay so still one knew that for them even to turn their heads was too much effort. Would Jimmy be lying still like the man in there? Would he be ghastly white like the boy in the next room? Would he be so swathed in bandages nobody could tell what he did look like? How could she bear it if his face was terribly burned!

At the entrance to a big room with several beds in it she faced another desk and another nurse. This one was more communicative than the one downstairs, probably because she had more to communicate. James Daniels was suffering from shock, partial smoke suffocation and exposure. He had extensive second-degree burns. His condition was slightly improved and the doctor now gave him an even chance.

Bonnie didn't know how bad second-degree burns were or just what the nurse meant by "shock" and "exposure." She did understand what "an even chance" meant.

The look in the girl's eyes seemed to disturb this nurse too. "His mother is with him. Would you like to speak to her?"

"No. I guess I won't bother her."

"Do you want me to give her a message?"

"No. Thank you."

What should she do now? Go home? There was a

four-o'clock boat from Broad Harbor in summer. She'd have to run to make it. But there was no use hanging around here if she couldn't see Jimmy. And it would be wonderful to see Ma!

She started to dash down the corridor to the elevator but slipped on the linoleum, which had been waxed and scrubbed to perilous smoothness. An arm shot out and kept her from falling. Two plump arms encircled her shoulders and a familiar voice said, "Bonnie Andrews, how on earth did you get here?"

She looked up into the face of Jimmy's mother and saw a smile that made her feel warm deep inside. Mrs. Daniels was actually glad to see her! The girl began to talk very fast. She told how she had happened to hear Jimmy's call for help over the radio, of her telephone calls and how she had taken the seven o'clock bus because she "simply had to know how he was."

"Oh, Bonnie, if only we can make Jimmy understand that you are here! He's out of his head and near's I can make out he thinks you're on the *Cormorant* and he's got to save you and can't get to you. Maybe if you came in and told him you were right here and all O.K. he'd understand and calm down. But I don't s'pose he'll know you. He doesn't know me."

They walked into the big room. Bonnie saw a light head on a pillow and went straight to that bed. Jimmy's sea-blue eyes stared up at her and through her with not the least sign of recognition. There was anxiety, terrible anxiety, in those eyes and they seemed to be looking out across miles of water.

"Hi, Jimmy," she said softly. "It's Bonnie."

His lips moved, but he was not speaking to her or to anybody else, only muttering unintelligible-sounding things to himself.

She picked up one of the broad, strong-fingered hands that lay so strangely idle on the bed. (Come to think of it, Jimmy's hands were never idle. When there was nothing else to do he whittled.)

Holding the hot, limp hand in her own, she said over and over, "It's Bonnie. I'm all right. I'm safe, Jimmy."

Still he strained to look into space. Still wrinkles pulled the eyebrows together above his troubled eyes.

"Sit down and keep right on talking," urged Mrs. Daniels. "I'll wait a little while in the room at the end of the hall."

So Bonnie sat there, holding the boy's hand and saying over and over the same things — that she was safe, that the Coast Guard picket boat had come for her. Then she had a sudden inspiration. "I'm here in

Secret Cove, Jimmy, all safe in *Secret Cove.*"

"Secret Cove!" he repeated to Bonnie's surprise.

"Yes, Jimmy. I'm here under — the big spruce — on the stone seat." She couldn't seem to keep those little breaks out of her voice. Secret Cove, with the big spruce and the stone seat and the toy village, was part of a happy time now gone. "Lift that branch and you'll see me, Jimmy. It's quiet and cool in here. Let's stay all afternoon. I don't have to go home till I hear the *Anne Marie* coming. Let's paint the — little toy — lighthouse."

Still holding his hand firmly in hers, she talked on, trying to pull Jimmy out of the dark waters where he floundered.

"Secret Cove," he murmured again, yet showed no sign of recognizing her.

"Yes, we're both safe in Secret Cove." She leaned over and kissed him gently on the forehead.

He did not speak again. His mother, coming back a few minutes later, gave a soft cry of surprise. "Look at him! He's asleep. Why, he's all calmed down."

Bonnie looked at the face on the pillow. The forehead had smoothed out. The lids had dropped down over the staring, worried eyes. The lips no longer moved.

"Visiting hour is over," announced a nurse, coming

into the ward on the stroke of the hour, like something run by electricity.

"And now you and I'd better have something to eat," suggested Mrs. Daniels. "We can come back at seven. How about your staying the night with me? I've got a room down the street here. Or have you got some other plans?"

Plans! Bonnie had none. She had forgotten hunger and thirst, forgotten that the boat left at four o'clock and that she had missed it and had no place to sleep. Seated at a lunch counter with a plate of fried haddock and potato in front of her, she developed a fisherman's appetite. It was almost twenty-four hours since she had eaten a regular meal.

"I don't know what you said to Jimmy, but you sure relieved his mind. Guess you've done more'n a doctor could for him," the older woman told her. "He'd got the notion into his head that you were drowning and he couldn't get to you to save you. Nothing I said made him think different."

"I told him I was safe in Secret Cove."

Jimmy was still asleep when they went back to the hospital.

Bonnie slept that night too.

"James Daniels had a comfortable night. His condition is improved," the nurse reported next morning when Jimmy's mother called the hospital.

She and Bonnie were almost gay at breakfast. They laughed like a couple of girls. The hundred-watt lights were on again in the girl's eyes.

The two wished the morning away. They began to wonder if the clock on the town hall was wrong, so slowly did the hours drag. Not till they looked at the one on the Broad Harbor Savings Bank and another in the post office could they believe that all of them were ticking along at their usual rate. "If I only could pitch in and clean house or do a big washing!" sighed Mrs. Daniels. "Then the time 'tween now and visiting hours would be a lot shorter." There was nothing to do but wander about Broad Harbor. They went in and out of stores but bought nothing. They walked up and down the residential streets and saw nobody they knew.

To be sure, Bonnie had many young friends here. Yet she was glad not to meet any of them. They would ask questions. They would want to hear all about her summer and how Jimmy was and what really had happened to him and so on. Maybe tomorrow she could talk — but not today. Mrs. Daniels understood how the girl felt. "I haven't been to see Jane Ellis — she was Jane Joyce, you know, before she got married. She'd want me to tell her all about what happened night before last and I just can't talk about it yet."

She hadn't even told Bonnie much about the catastrophe — just the barest facts. That Jimmy and Fred Murphy's two boys had gone out together deep-sea fishing, that there had been an explosion and the boat had caught fire, that the Murphy boys, who were both younger than Jimmy, had lost their heads, that Jimmy had kept at the radiotelephone, half-suffocated from smoke and badly burned, and sent out call after call for help — those calls Bonnie had heard — that the three had managed to hang on to the sides of the boat, with just their heads and shoulders out of water till the Coast Guard picket boat arrived.

Jimmy's mother, though she couldn't talk much about the accident, could and did talk about Jimmy — the good job he had at Murphy's boatshop, how he said this and said that. She even went back across the years and related little-boy doings and sayings. Bonnie listened a bit absently. She was asking herself disturbing questions. Would Jimmy be conscious? Would he know her? Would he remember that he and his former girl friend were no longer friends? Would he turn on her that frozen look?

The morning ended at last. Again the stout, middle-aged woman and the slip of a seventeen-year-old girl stood beside Jimmy's bed. They thought at first he was asleep. He lay perfectly still, with his eyes closed. Then the lids opened slowly. Gone was the far-off stare. "Hi, Ma!" The voice was a husky imitation of Jimmy Daniels's voice. Then he saw Bonnie and stared unbelievingly.

He must hear my heart beating, thought the girl. Wasn't he going to say *anything?* Words came at last — slowly.

"You're — really — here, Bonnie?"

"Yes, Jimmy, I'm really here."

"That wasn't a dream I had?"

"No. I came yesterday and talked to you."

"She came all the way back from Massachusetts specially to see you," added his mother.

Jimmy smiled. The girl looking down at him suddenly realized that no one she had ever seen in her whole life had a smile like Jimmy's.

"Back again? What kind of a time did you have up there in the hills?" asked Captain Taylor when he collected Bonnie's fare on the boat the next day. He spoke casually, as if she had been away but a short time.

"An Even Chance"

It really *was* a short time, she had to remind her-self, less than six weeks, no more than half a summer. It seemed like a year, so much had happened. It seemed that she must look at least a year older than the girl who went away at the end of June carrying this same suitcase, wearing this same dress.

With the eyes of one who has been absent a long time, she watched the familiar islands rise out of the sea. Surely this world of water and islands and boats and sea birds had never looked quite so beauti-ful. Even the harsh cries of the gulls as they followed the trail of the mail boat were sweet to her ears today. She counted off the islands one by one — Long Island, Black Island, Gull Island, Goose Island, Seal Island. She was almost there. Wouldn't the folks be surprised to see her? They didn't expect her till next week.

A knot of people stood as usual on the Bayberry Harbor wharf to watch the mail boat come in. The girl in the pink dress scanned each figure. Ma or Pa or the kids might just happen to be here.

"Hi, Bonnie Jean." A brown arm shot up in the air and waved wildly above a golden-brown head.

It was Greg. Why, she hadn't thought of him for weeks. She hadn't even answered his last two letters. He was smiling a big smile. Yet Bonnie wished he were not here. He would insist on carrying her suit-case and walking home with her. He would want to walk slowly and talk a mile a minute. She wanted to get home in a hurry. He would ask all about Music Hill and she didn't feel like talking about Music Hill tonight. He would inquire, oh so politely, how Jimmy was getting along, but wouldn't care at all. He would press invitations upon her. There were just five people she wanted to see tonight and they all lived together in a little house in Pretty Cove.

The boat drew closer to the landing. The captain turned off the engine. At the rear of the wharf there was a lobster car — a large tank for storing lobsters until they were shipped to the markets. A big-framed man stood dumping a tubful of lobsters into the car. He wore faded, stained khaki pants and a much-darned cardigan topped by an ancient, shapeless felt hat.

"Pa! Pa!" shouted Bonnie. "It's me. I'm home!"

26. August Days Are Short Days

THE *Summer Wind* rocked gently. A soft breeze fanned the three people who sat on deck eating lunch under a red- and white-striped awning.

"It was a wonderful experience," said Bonnie gravely. "I shall never forget it."

Mrs. Watson's face shone. "I *knew* you'd love Music Hill. Tell us *all* about it."

How could she "tell all about" Music Hill in a few minutes or even in an hour? And how could she possibly make these two people understand what that experience had meant to her?

"Did you have fun?" put in Greg.

"No, not fun. What I had I guess were growing pains."

"You had *what?*"

"Growing pains. I'm not a child any more. And I'm not daydreaming any more."

"Gee whiz! let me count your gray hairs, Bonnie." Why couldn't Greg see that she was very serious?

"You poor dear! Was it as bad as that?"

"No, Mrs. Watson, it was good. I needed just what I found at Music Hill, growing pains and all."

"Those long-hairs probably made you feel like a worm." The boy sounded indignant now.

She shook her head emphatically. "They didn't. They were grand. I was an Alice in Wonderland. First I drank something that made me feel very small and uncomfortable. Then I ate something that made me feel big and important — I mean part of big, important things, part of a world full of — Oh, I'm afraid I can't quite tell you how Music Hill did make me feel," she added at sight of the two puzzled faces turned toward her. They looked the way the twins looked sometimes when they listened to older people talking. Why, these two, she thought, are both really younger than I am, even if Mrs. Watson is fortyish and Greg seventeen. People grew up at different speeds. She knew that now. Look at Ernestine Mannheimer — at twenty-one an old woman in experience.

"I guess you were pretty homesick," said Mrs. Watson, trying to make sense out of what the girl said.

"After the first week, I was hardly homesick at all."

Mrs. Watson gave up and changed the subject. "Did Greg write you about the trip we're going to take on the *Summer Wind?* You're coming, aren't you?"

"I'm terribly sorry, Mrs. Watson, but I don't see how I can go away again before school begins."

"Of course she's going, Mother." It was the same old Greg who wouldn't take "No" for an answer.

He walked across the Point with Bonnie, walked slowly, talking all the way.

"I can't possibly go," she kept saying. "Don't you see I can't after I've been away all summer?"

No, he couldn't see why she would turn down a week's cruise on the *Summer Wind*. Didn't she want to go? Had she forgotten what fun they had last year? Well, it was going to be the same bunch and they'd have just as much fun.

Yes, she wanted to go. No, she hadn't forgotten last year.

She spoke mechanically and Greg suddenly burst out, "What's got into you, Bonnie? Did you fall for some long-hair at Music Hill?"

"No. I didn't fall for anybody at Music Hill. It's just that I have to help Ma and get my clothes ready for school and do a lot of things."

He refused to take such reasons seriously. The conversation turned into an argument in which Greg kept saying with more and more bitterness, "You don't want to go," and Bonnie repeated doggedly, "I do *so,* I do *so.*"

Even as she disputed him the girl knew that he was right. The lovely *Summer Wind* had lost its lure. Greg, with his golden sun-tan, his flowery shirts which never seemed to fade and his gay laugh which never lost its gaiety, could not wave a wand now and turn her into a dream companion and take her with him into a dream. He could not make her feel excited and out of breath any more.

Finally Bonnie came out with her big reason for staying at home. It was Jimmy. He would be back from the hospital in a few days, and she wanted to welcome him home and see all she could of him between now and September.

"So it's that dr —" A glance at her face prevented him from calling Jimmy either a "drip" or a "droop."

234

"So it's the boatbuilder. I *knew* it was *somebody*."

"Yes. It's the boatbuilder."

"I ought to have seen you were *that way* about him. Well, good-by, Bonnie Jean." He turned and went along the path and did not look back or wave.

Bonnie was suddenly reminded of something that had happened one day a few years before. In the midst of a southwest gale there had appeared in Pretty Cove a handsome bird. No one but Henry Mc-Adam had ever seen one like it before. He recalled having seen a flock of those same birds off the Virginia coast when he was down there in the Coast Guard. The visitor had sat out the storm hunched up in the lee of a high rock. Next morning, when Bonnie ran down to the cove, the bird was gone. She had hoped hard that he reached Virginia all right, for he did not seem to belong on a rock-rimmed northern island. No more did Greg.

"That Watson boy's just a big kid," she exclaimed to her mother when she got home.

"He always was," said Ma, "but you've been too much of a kid yourself to know it — till now."

On Monday the Bayberry Island girl stood in Pretty Cove and watched the *Summer Wind* spread white sails to the breeze and vanish around Cranberry Point. The schooner would come winging back in a week. It would keep coming back to anchor in this cove. Yet Bonnie knew that it had sailed out of her life never to return.

"I sure will," said Bonnie.

This time she was not talking to Greg Watson. She was sitting on the beach at Pretty Cove. Jimmy was stretched out in the sun beside her. He had come home to convalesce and was doing most of it not at his own home but at Bonnie's. His hands were busy, carving out of a block of wood a new boat model for the twins. Bonnie's hands were busy too, making buttonholes and sewing buttons on the new plaid wool dress Ma had made for her.

"That's sharp," said Jimmy.

They had talked steadily all the August afternoon, making up for a year lost. It was more than a year since the two had talked together and gone put-putting about in the *Water Spider*. There was much to tell each other, and there were some things to get out of each other's heads. Jimmy, for instance, seemed to have a fixed idea that Bonnie cared a lot about Greg Watson. It took much talk to convince him that she didn't. "I never felt like Bonnie Jean Andrews when I was with him. I felt as if I were play-acting or something. It wasn't really *me*. That boat didn't seem real either."

"What about his kisses? Weren't those real?"

"We-ell, he did kiss me once. It was real all right, but I never cared much for that kiss."

He threw back his head and laughed at this, and that laughter cleared the air.

There was something on Bonnie's mind too. What about Mary Lunt?

Jimmy laughed again, this time at the thought of his being interested in Mary. "That was when *I* did some play-acting. Wanted to make you jealous."

"Anyway, you kissed her."

"I never kissed Mary in my life. Who told you such a lie as that?"

"The same person who told you about Greg's kissing me."

"Mabel Collins!"

The fog banks between them all vanished.

They went on talking. He told about the job he had now at Murphy's boatshop. It was good pay and he was going to save and save so that in a few years he could have his own business around here somewhere. "Fred says I have a very special knack for boatbuilding."

"*I* knew that a long time ago," said Bonnie.

She told about Music Hill and the "growing pains" and feeling older, and he understood exactly how she felt. He had had those pains — in Boston. She talked about being a senior and about graduating next June, and how she wanted to go to the state teachers' college at Bellport. "I think now I'll teach music in schools," she said.

Jimmy had one more thing on his mind, something he had wondered about all the while he was in the hospital. Had he dreamed that she kissed him that time or had she really kissed him?

"I really kissed you."

Then he smiled one of his very best smiles and asked, "Would you show me just how you did it?"

It was then that Bonnie said, "I sure will."

After that they talked of the future — of its certainties and uncertainties. He might within the year be called into the service. He might be sent to the other side of the world to fight. But always he would come back to Bayberry Island, at least if she would wait for him.

"Yes, Jimmy, I'll wait."

They didn't talk much after that. They just sat there in the sunshine. A great certainty shone in their faces — the certainty that each loved the other.

27. The Launching of the *Bonnie Jean*

MURPHY's big, barnlike boatshop in Easton was all dressed up for a celebration. The floor, swept clean of sawdust, shavings and pieces of wood, offered no threat to dainty shoes. The big saws, planes and all movable machinery had been pushed back into corners to make room for company. The place was crowded with men, women and children, come to see the launching.

A long table covered with a flowered cloth was the center of attention for the children. On it were set out plates of cakes and cookies, and pitchers that tinkled tantalizingly when anybody jiggled the table.

For the grown folks, interest was centered on the new forty-two foot seiner, still sitting in the wooden cradle in which it had been built. For one girl, the center of interest on that boat was the name painted across the prow: *Bonnie Jean.*

All signs showed that at almost any moment now the *Bonnie Jean* would go down the ways. The tide was right. Ropes had been tied to boat and cradle and to the wharf. Men stood by with great hammers ready to knock away the blocks and braces that held cradle and seiner from slipping. The ways under the cradle were heavily greased. From the prow hung a bottle as gay as a Christmas package, wrapped in tinsel paper and tied with ribbons.

At the prow stood Bonnie, easily the prettiest thing in sight, wearing a white dress with a corsage of pink rosebuds. The dress was the one she had worn the week before at her graduation from Broad Harbor High School. The corsage, presented to her by Mr. Murphy, marked her as the important person who was to christen the seiner.

The *Bonnie Jean* was in a sense Jimmy's boat and

always would be, although it was about to become the property of somebody else. Jimmy had been in charge of building her and he was almost bursting with pride over the trim, graceful but sturdy craft turned out. He had been asked to name her, because, as the owner said, "She's your girl." The boatbuilder promptly came up with *Bonnie Jean*.

The girl felt terribly responsible. She had to break that bottle at exactly the right moment or the boat would get away from her. When the blocks were knocked out and the *Bonnie Jean* began to slide, it would go like greased lightning. And not to be properly christened was the worst possible luck for a boat. She had heard Mr. Murphy tell of the launching of the *Sea Pigeon*. That seiner got away and plunged into the sea before the christener did the job and everything bad that could happen to a boat befell that poor *Pigeon*.

The men raised their heavy hammers. "O.K., Bonnie," called Jimmy, his voice full of excitement.

Grasping the bottle firmly by its beribboned neck, she shut her eyes and gave a mighty whack. The boat was christened — none too soon. With a rush, boat and cradle plunged into the sea. A mighty splash announced that the *Bonnie Jean* had gone down the ways and begun her life as a seagoing boat.

Bonnie, Island Girl

Bonnie stood on the dock and watched her namesake cutting easily and confidently through the water, heading straight for the channel and the open sea on her trial run. Jimmy stood beside Bonnie. "She may have to go through some awful storms," he said. "She can't have it all fair weather and following winds. But I'm betting my last dollar on her. She has a fine Diesel engine. She's a good boat, built to stand all the tests the old sea can give her."

"Good luck, *Bonnie Jean*," said the girl softly.

"Good luck!" echoed the boy.

Both were wishing themselves as well as the boat good luck in the uncertain years ahead.

They stood there together after the other guests had gone and the big shop behind them was empty. They stared out across the water long after the seiner had turned into a speck and disappeared behind an island.